THE ROCK POOL

CYRIL VERNON CONNOLLY, born in Coventry in 1903, was the son of a professional soldier, who, when he retired from the army, became a renowned conchologist. Connolly was educated, as a Colleger, at Eton, where he earned a remarkable reputation for social wit and intellectual daring. From Eton he went up with a scholarship to Balliol College, Oxford, where again he made his mark. His academic record, however, was mediocre; and his prospects seemed uncertain, until Desmond MacCarthy, then literary editor of the *New Statesman*, prompted him to write reviews, and Logan Pearsall-Smith engaged him as his scholarly assistant. Then, in 1930, he married, and spent much of the next seven or eight years travelling around Europe. His only novel, *The Rock Pool*, was published in 1936, and *Enemies of Promise*, the long critical and autobiographical survey that established his adult fame, in 1938. *The Unquiet Grave*, part personal confession, part a series of acute reflections upon life and art, came out in 1944. In 1950, having resigned his editorship of *Horizon*, the avant-garde monthly magazine he had helped to found in 1939, he adopted literary journalism as a means of livelihood, served briefly as the *Observer*'s literary editor, and from 1951, for the remainder of his life, contributed weekly to the columns of *The Sunday Times*. His later works include four volumes of collected essays, among them *The Condemned Playground* and *Ideas and Places*. A man with many friends and admirers, he died in 1974.

PETER QUENNELL was born in 1905. He was educated at Berkhamsted School and Balliol College where he began a friendship with Cyril Connolly that was to last for over fifty years. His books include studies of Byron, Ruskin, Hogarth, Shakespeare, and Pope, as well as three autobiographical volumes, *The Sign of the Fish*, *The Marble Foot* and *The Wanton Chase*. He edited *History Today* from 1951 to 1979.

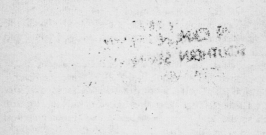

CYRIL CONNOLLY

The Rock Pool

———«‹◇›»———

WITH AN INTRODUCTION BY
PETER QUENNELL

A dolor! ibat Hylas, ibat Hamadryasin

45661

New York
PERSEA BOOKS
1981

TO PETER QUENNELL

Copyright © 1981 by Deidre Levi
New Introduction Copyright © 1981 by Peter Quennell
All rights reserved
For information, address the publisher:
Persea Books, Inc.
225 Lafayette Street
New York, N.Y. 10012
International Standard Book Number: 0–89255–059–7
Library of Congress Catalog Card Number: 81–82928

First edition

Printed in Great Britain

INTRODUCTION

BY PETER QUENNELL

CYRIL CONNOLLY was a generous donor of books, though the books he had casually borrowed he did not always trouble to return; and presentation-copies of those he had himself written often bore a friendly message, reminding me, for example, when I received *The Unquiet Grave*, that I had known 'the places and the people', and quoting a Latin poet's line about the '*amarum aliquid*', the touch of something bitter, that 'rises to torment us even among the flowers themselves'.* *Enemies of Promise* is also flatteringly inscribed: 'Peter from Cyril, on the rough anniversary of a friendship which has lasted fifteen terrifying years'. The date was November 1938; and we had met at Oxford, where we were both scholars of Balliol, in October 1923.

Since we left Oxford, our paths had frequently diverged. Cyril had spent a good deal of his time travelling around Europe, while my own career, except for a longish visit to Japan, had been largely based on London. But I had watched his progress; and, whenever he reappeared, I had much enjoyed his company, his gossip and marvellous sense of fun and his stimulating discursions upon life and art. Of all my Oxford friends I regarded him as the cleverest and, if the circumstances were right and his mood serene, certainly the most amusing.

Given such talents, however, I occasionally asked myself, why did Cyril not write more? Perhaps his existence was too easy, a little too pleasantly arranged. In 1930 he

*See Lucretius, *De Rerum Natura, IV*

had married a charming American girl, who was not only intelligent but sympathetic and responsive, and provided the modest financial support that enabled them to cultivate the tastes they shared – for travel, hospitality, excellent food and wine, Mediteranean landscapes and the custody of strange, delightful pets. Their alliance, until their playgrounds were condemned, and the atmosphere of the 1930s grew more and more disturbing, seemed – at least from the outsider's point of view – an unusually well-balanced marriage.

It was half-way through these happy wander-years that Cyril wrote his first and last novel, which, after various reverses, came out in 1936, to be followed in 1938 by *Enemies of Promise*, the critical and autobiographical excursion that definitely made his name. Not that *The Rock Pool* failed to attract notice. Of the American edition Edmund Wilson observed that, although the story 'owes something to *South Wind* and Compton Mackenzie's novels of Capri', it 'differs from them through its acceleration, which, as in the wildly speeded-up burlesques, has something demoniacal about it'. Desmond MacCarthy, reviewing the English edition, was even more enthusiastic; he described the book as 'a theme admirably and seriously handled, and as a novel written with peremptory and witty precision, and a spirited, off-hand elegance extremely pleasing'.

Cyril's severest critics were a brace of English publishers to whom he had begun by offering it. One of them had first accepted the manuscript, but then abruptly turned it down – at the instigation, we heard, of a senior partner, who happened to find lesbianism a peculiarly painful topic. The other, as Cyril explains in his dedicatory epistle, announced that it couldn't possibly be published 'over here' and would appeal, if it appealed at all, to a sophisticated minority. Each firm deplored the narrative's 'tone' and its lack of moral weight. Cyril then despaired – he was always apt to give up hope – and approached a Continental publisher, the engaging but 'faintly mephisto-lean Jack Kahane', proprietor of the Parisian Obelisk Press, who, far from regretting its tone, declared that its Anglo-Saxon reticence positively disgraced his list. Finally, the novel reached London, and was reissued by Hamish Hamilton, a learned and enlightened member of his trade, in the year 1947.

That *The Rock Pool* should ever have been judged obscene may astonish modern readers. It contains none of those embarrassing descriptions of the physical joys of love which the most popular English and American novel-ists now insert to brighten up their pages, and gives, on the whole, a fairly sinister account of the guilty passions it describes. Cyril did not pretend to be a moralist, but was concerned with characters he had met, their effect on his literary imagination, and scenes that he had closely stud-ied. At the same time, the subject he dealt with was the clash between two cultures – the snobbish, cliché-ridden English world that his unhappy hero represents and what remained, he thought, of ancient pagan society among the dissolute inhabitants of Trou-sur-Mer, people who obsti-nately 'did their own thing' and continued to gratify their coarse primaeval instincts.

Cyril's novel is not a *roman-à-clef* in the ordinary mean-ing of the term; but its background and many of its person-ages are distinctly recognizable. I, too, have visited Trou-sur-Mer (better known as Cagnes), and have climbed the street that leads from a tawdry seaside suburb to the ancient hill-town; and Cyril once showed me a small faded photograph of the girl he renamed Sonia – or was it her beloved companion Toni? – seated, I suppose, at the local bus-stop, her chin despondently cupped in her hands, on a rather battered piece of luggage.

As for Naylor, the conceited and pretentious young Englishman, who arrives to look and patronize, but, at length, like the antique Hylas, is sucked down into the rock pool, the postcript that Cyril wrote soon after the War claims that he had two originals. I can recognize only one – an old friend whose amatory mishaps were somewhat similar to Naylor's, though his good qualities – he would die an heroic death in a 'black winter night above Germany' – for the purposes of the story have, he says, been 'ruthlessly suppressed'. The painter Rascasse never came my way. When the War had reached the South of France, with his pride and peasant industry and 'reptilian tenacity of life' he alone survived the deluge. His memorial is a joint portrait of Cyril and Jean Connolly – not, I am afraid, a very good picture – that used to hang in Cyril's rooms.

These diverse characters fascinated the novelist; but the whole community, viewed as a social phenomenon, he clearly found no less engrossing. They were a doomed tribe:

Even Juan-les-Pins seemed non-existent after the mysterious jungle atmosphere of Trou-sur-Mer; people there seemed to live an intense nocturnal life, to be as shy of observation as an Indian reserve near a densely populated city. . . . They resembled the Chleuhs of the Atlas, wild, gloomy freedom-loving tribesmen whom the French hemmed in and starved into surrender. Theirs was the Bled Siba, the *pays de dissidence* where the hopelessness of the struggle was admitted with fatalism, yet where all fought on.

At this point, it may perhaps be objected that the novelist romanticized his raw material – a gang of rampageous bohemians, neither brilliant nor dignified, quarrelsome, dishonest, crafty, living from drink to drink, and bed to bed. But then, Cyril was a great romantic; and a romantic he remained until the end. True, he resented the label, and

would sometimes lose his temper if I quoted Shelley's
verses –

> We look before and after,
> And pine for what is not:
> Our sincerest laughter
> With some pain is fraught. . . .

– and suggested they might possibly apply to him. His
favourite authors, he declared, were Catullus, Tibullus,
Juvenal, Petronius and, in English, Congreve, Rochester,
Dryden and Pope, all of whom had been brought up on the
classical tradition.

Despite these influences, however, Cyril's romanticism
pervaded his life and helped to shape his work. He was
constantly regretting the past and dreaming of some future
period, when all his aspirations would be fulfilled and his
brightest visions realized. Regret and nostalgia were the
emotions he appears to have felt most strongly and, in his
books, expressed most vividly; and *The Unquiet Grave*,
written while he was a war-time exile, cut off from the
faraway scenes he loved, is a lament for abandoned hopes
and lost illusions.

Twice he had nearly achieved contentment – at Eton,
where, like Byron at Harrow, he had enjoyed his Golden
Age, and when he was first married and sought to put into
practice his romantic 'concept of life as an arrogant private
dream shared by two'. But even at that period his mood
was frequently restless: 'in one lovely place (Palinurus
admits) always pining for another; with the perfect woman
imagining one more perfect. . .'. Cyril and his wife adored
the South of France; but 'Living for Beauty', he explains,
involved a busy routine of 'answering advertisements, for
information about cottages in Hampstead, small manors
in the West – or else for portable canoes, converted Dutch
barges . . . second-hand yachts, caravans and cars'. They

were happy enough; yet perfect happiness still awaited them around the corner.

This strain of emotional ambivalence runs through almost everything he wrote. As Catullus had done, he loved and hated; and the Mediterranean itself, to which he had owed so much enjoyment, in *The Rock Pool* is denounced by his hero (behind whom seems to lurk the novelist) as a dismal sink of vice and ennui:

The intolerable melancholy, the dinginess, the corruption of that tainted inland sea overcame him. He felt the breath of centuries of wickedness and disillusion; how many civilizations had staled on that bright promontory! Sterile Phoenicians, commercial-minded Greeks, destructive Arabs, Catalans, Genoese, hysterical Russians, decayed English, drunken Americans, had mingled with the autochthonous gangsters – everything that was vulgar, acquisitive, piratical . . . had united there. . . .

Compare this passage with the nostaligic memories he recalled in one of the most evocative sections of *The Unquiet Grave*:

Early morning on the Mediterranean: bright air resinous with Aleppo pine, water spraying over the gleaming tarmac of the Route Nationale and darkly reflecting the spring-summer green of the planes; swifts wheeling round the oleander . . . armfuls of carnations on the flower-stall. . . . Now cooks from many yachts step ashore with their market-baskets, one-eyed cats scrounge among the fish-heads, while the hot sun refracts the dancing sea-glitter on the café awning, until the sea becomes a green gin-fizz of stillness in whose depths a quiver of sprats charges and counter-charges in the pleasure of fishes.

The Rock Pool illustrates both attitudes towards Trou-sur-Mer and its inhabitants. Among these dingy outcasts Naylor sights two young girls, Toni and Sonia, embodiments of youth and beauty, and feels that, whatever their moral defects may be, he is 'in the presence of something noble and elegiac'. But then, inevitably, he becomes aware of the *amarum aliquid*:

Alas, how miserable their good looks made him! The pain of watching beautiful young girls, the isolation of desire! They reminded him of the figures in one of those pictures by Watteau that are instinct with the beauty of the moment, the fugitive distress of hedonism, the sadness that falls like dew from pleasure, as they stand, fixed in the movement of the dance, beneath the elms, beneath the garlanded urn.

Besides revealing the romantic and nostalgic aspects of Cyril's nature, *The Rock Pool* has another quality; it displays his satirical wit and unfailing grasp of the cruelly descriptive image. Trou's only rich inhabitant is a certain Mr Foster, who pretends to be a Wykehamist and, for some unknown reason, wears a kilt. He has a neglected American wife:

She was a not unattractive, embittered young woman, speaking his own language of little digs and understatements. She had done her hair in a different way and was braving her husband's unrelenting disapproval. He would stare at her coiffure silently, then manage a sort of unconscious wince, as if he were thinking of something else and only the protesting muscles of his face were aware of her. He treated Naylor with old-world discourtesy.

The conflict between these two Englishmen – one rather uneasily vain of his superior social standing, and of the fact that he is a genuine Wykehamist and once belonged to a famous Oxford college; while the other, though financially more secure, has had a slightly less distinguished past – provokes some splendid comic dialogues. Asked what he did at Cambridge, Foster claims that he had played 'paolo'; at which Naylor, who fears and detests horses ('those fierce, inscrutable creatures'), decides that he must change the subject:

After all, as the challenged, he had choice of weapons.
'Really? What fun. What college were you at?'
'Sidney Sussex'.
He's on the hop.
'I'm afraid I don't know anyone there – were there any Wykeham-ists?'
'Nao – were you at Winchester?'
'Yes – where were you?'
Groggy – can't last.
'Berkhamsted'.
'Oh, yes, I've heard of it – it's very healthy, isn't it?'

The Rock Pool, among its various themes, is an attack on the English social system and the crass competitiveness that it engenders; and, describing the history of the book in the letter he addressed to me, Cyril records that 'it was originally to have formed the middle panel of a triptych, one of three studies in English snobbery; but it outgrew the other two stories which dealt with the London and County forms of the disease. . .'. Cyril was neither a snob himself nor determinedly competitive; but I suspect that he was deeply emulous, and that he must often, so long as he lived abroad, have been a little annoyed by the news of English life, and of their own recent successes, that he received from former friends, as is Naylor when a clever Oxford associate sends him a teasingly phrased account of all the fun that he is missing.

To equate Naylor with the novelist would, I believe, be totally mistaken; but there seems no doubt that certain traces of Cyril – his over-sensitiveness, his pride, his ambitions and his romantic day-dreams – have been transferred to Naylor's personality; and the ill-fated hero, in so far as he has an independent existence, is the least satisfactory feature of the book. This weakness did not escape Cyril. 'The fault I am most conscious of . . . is that of dating,' he wrote; every first book is 'the settlement of a debt with

the past, and . . . my debt is with the nineteen-twenties . . .
a period when art was concerned with futility, when
heroes were called Denis and Nigel and Stephen, and had a
tortured look'. He thought he might claim, he added, that
he had 'created a young man as futile as any'; and futility is
a disintegrating attribute in the presentation of a character. Like Flaubert's Frédéric in *L'Éducation Sentimentale*
– a nineteenth-century portrayal of a thoroughly ineffec-
tive young man – Naylor is a personage to whom 'things
happen' and disastrous calamities occur, but who remains
their passive prey.

Otherwise, granted these shortcomings, *The Rock Pool*,
seen as a prentice novel, is a remarkably well-constructed
story, that carries us swiftly along from Naylor's
appearance in Trou until the moment, on the hotel terrace,
of his supreme humiliation. 'Just another bum', the
English tourists decide, and hasten to avoid his clutches.
The book is a tragi-comedy and a poetic threnody combined, shot through by dazzling gleams of humour.

That it should have been Cyril's only novel, though he
occasionally sketched in a successor, is not difficult to
understand. He needed a strong emotional stimulus, such
as his adventures at Cagnes had given him; and then, he
was an aesthetic idealist and a literary perfectionist. Once
he had returned to London, the gloomy war-years had
begun and his happy marriage broke up, he became an
editor and regular reviewer. These occupations sharpened
his critical sense, until it had developed a self-destructive
edge; and his high standards he applied not only to the
work of others, but to his own imaginative projects, often
fatally checking them in mid-career.

His admirers expected much of Cyril; of himself he
expected even more, and was sometimes poignantly dis-
appointed; so that, after *The Rock Pool* and *Enemies of
Promise*, *The Unquiet Grave* alone – a cry of regret and

remorse, a 'signal of distress', that the recipient, he tells us, never answered – seemed fully worthy of his gifts. Yet his literary reputation grew despite his lapses into silence. Cyril impressed himself on his contemporaries, and excited vigorous praise and blame, as few English writers of his period have done; and his three major books each added something to the extraordinary self-portrait that, with its wit and imaginative insight and unselfconscious analysis of his radically divided nature, I cannot help thinking was his great achievment. A hundred years hence, it will still attract readers who wish to penetrate the background of the troubled twentieth century; and in *The Rock Pool* they will observe the artist's hand starting work upon his canvas.

London 1981.

Dear Peter,

It is a simple matter to dedicate to you the book which you encouraged me to finish. But there are still one or two things I would like to say about it. After the brief and disconcerting attention it received from the publishers I find myself wondering how far I am to blame, to what I owe the streak of 'unpleasantness', the infirmity of 'moral tone' which they found so unacceptable, and if I have, perhaps, gone through all my life so far with an imagination and a code of ethics more depraved than anyone else's. Thinking it over, I ascribe this moral infection to my schooldays, and more especially to the use of cribs. At my school there existed a tradition of classical learning. Although we went to chapel every morning and had prayers every evening, and two lots of chapel and two sets of prayers on Sunday, and answered questions ranging from the difference between Jehoiakim and Jehoiakin to the reasons why Tertullian became a Montanist, nevertheless the greater part of our working day was spent in learning Latin. For twenty-four hours Christianity became the official religion, but the week-day god whom with the help of the officiating staff we struggled to cultivate was Horace. Since we were mostly engrossed with games and gossip, we did not carry the worship very far, but it was then that we were in the greatest danger. Under the usual system of teaching Latin which prevails in our public schools it is not possible for an ordinary boy ever to grasp the meaning of anything he translates. He construes laboriously from word to word and in his fear of missing one of the stepping-stones to which he has to hop, he has no time to consider the beauties of the river. But many of us had no time for the stepping-stones, and so we were tempted to make use of a crib, an 'illegal rendering'. Cribs were of two kinds: pretentious and extremely free translations in verse, to which access was easy, but whose help was negligible; and word for word translations published by Kelly and Bohn, which employed such a remote and extraordinary vocabulary that anyone consulting them was still wholesomely far from appreciating the quality of the original. But in my time there appeared another kind of translation. This was the Loeb classical library, which printed a prose version of the Latin beside the original, and which, won as a prize by one's fagmaster, was available, by unwritten law, for the use of his slaves. From that moment one could no longer (I was now in my tenth year of learning Latin) spend hours over an author without discovering what he was like. And the knowledge was poison. Several of us began to understand what we read, and to find out that we had been learning by heart the mature, ironical, sensual and irreligious opinions of a middle-aged Roman, one whose chief counsel to youth was to drink and make love to the best of its ability, as these were activities unsuitable to a middle age given over to wordly-wise meditation and good talk. Afterwards there remained only an equal oblivion for the virtuous and the wicked in the unconsulted tomb. Once embarked on these discoveries we extended them with passion and soon found out other pagan doctrines even more insolent in the passages which we were taught. Tacitus, Suetonius, Juvenal, Martial, Catullus and even Petronius were among the writers whom the authorities, confident in the immunity which their method of teaching bestowed, included in the curriculum, and we were also able to find a master whose mind was naturally Roman, and who confirmed us in what we had thought. Henceforth the invective of Catullus, the bile of Juvenal, and the aristocratic bawdy of Petronius became the natural food of our imaginations, the words 'cynical and irreverent' began to appear regularly in my reports and, though a romantic period was to follow, the seeds of a philosophy of life were sown, a philosophy indelibly tinged with materialism, robust, arrogant, sensible, deriving from the natural glamour of 'the smoke and *wealth and noise of Rome' where we now had our being, a philo-sophy not without elevation and melancholy, but unsuitable for the many Sundays which were to follow, for the cultivation of sexual abstinence and sexual intolerance, and for the place which it was hoped we would take in a democratic and modestly industrious world. When I afterwards came to enjoy my favourite English writers, who owed so much to those Latin originals, Congreve, Rochester, Dryden and Pope, I had already sunk so far that in either their language or opinions I could never find anything at which to take exception, and it is, I fear, this obtuseness, this insensitiveness to the horrors of wenching that gives the outrageous 'tone' to my book. A typical sentence, indeed, which a publisher requested me to alter, was: 'I want to have somebody tonight' into 'I don't want to be alone tonight' – as now it stands.*

As for the history of the book, you know it. It was originally to have formed the middle panel of a triptych, one of three studies in English snobbery, but it outgrew the other two stories which dealt with the London and County forms of the disease, and, perhaps because it was planned as a study in inverted snobbery between two normal ones, it finally absorbed them. The book was first accepted by one publisher, then promptly rejected by his partners, the Boy *and* Bessie Cotter *prosecutions intervening. The next publisher returned it, saying that it could not possibly be published over here, and in any case would only 'appeal to a few people' (the first compliment it has so far received). He had painstakingly pencilled round all the passages which he thought unsuitable, and looking over the manuscript, with the wavy pencil lines at first scanty, then growing as it seemed interminable, and finally almost breaking off in despair, I decided I might as well throw it away, that I was an altogether hopeless case. I know there is a theory that a book, if it is any good, will always find a publisher, that talent cannot be stifled, that it even proves itself by thriving on disappointment, but I have never subscribed to it; we do not expect spring flowers to bloom in a black frost, and I think the chill wind that blows from English publishers, with their black suits and thin umbrellas, and their habit of beginning every sentence with 'We are afraid', has nipped off more promising buds than it has strengthened.*

Most writers, of course, are not greatly hampered by the question of obscenity; there are a great many subjects they can write about which are unconnected with it, and much they can suggest without descending to a treatment which is too direct. Even so, I think the fear of obscenity must influence writers more deeply than they know, and cause sometimes a subconscious and fundamental castration of thought and feeling which is much more dangerous than the elisions of a publisher's pencil, and may well be responsible for the spinster fancies that are so enormously saleable. But there is a problem far greater and far more widespread than that of obscenity which must be solved by the English novelist – the question of libel. The writer of fiction does not create character. It is possible that the writer of genius does, but for most authors there is only one way to write a novel, and that is to put their friends, or other people they are in a position to observe, into it, and afterwards remove the labels as best they can. No novelist, of course, should wish his characters to be identified, and often, as in Proust, they are artistically improved by being blended with others, and by having all sorts of liberties taken with them; but it is equally true to say that even more characters are deformed by the retouching necessary to avoid libel actions: dates have to be altered, places disguised, painters turned into poets, names may have to be changed for the third or fourth time, and an institution like a school, which is often the most deserving subject for criticism or the richest in fictional possibilities, is too dangerous to be handled by the novelist at all. The result is that a blight is descending on the English novel. The dictatorship of the libraries (who circulate sensationalism but discourage realism), the fear of prosecutions for obscenity based often on quite irrespon-sible complaints (Bournemouth has just banned The Blue Lagoon *by Stacpoole) or of costly libel actions and expensive boycotts has driven the publishers into a state approaching panic, a panic which is transmitted to the author in terms of vexation, until the poor novelist proceeds down his road in blinkers, occasionally attempting to get away on to the path with something, a stroke of observation perhaps, but immediately being goaded back. These are among the reasons why, when it became possible for me to publish this book in Paris without any bother, I came to regard it as a good thing. I did not have to go through it again altering and emending, or trying to turn men into women and women into men. It did not even matter that it was too short, for, again due to the subversity of Latin, I have been trained rather to condense than to amplify and consequently to produce a book of the exact length on which all publishers wage war.*

Of course, my problems in writing this book have been different from those of anyone who thought of publishing it. I am not concerned with obscenity and libel but with the attempt to create character and manage dialogue, with the fear of anyone who has reviewed a lot of books that they are themselves hopelessly sterile ('Those who can't, teach!') and consequently my personal triumph is to have written a book at all. If one has criticized novels for several years one is supposed to have profited from them. Actually one finds one's mind irremediably silted up with every trick and cliché, every still-born phrase and facile and second-hand expression that one has deplored in others. The easy trade of reviewing is found to have carried banality with it to the point of an occupational disease. The fault I am most conscious of, besides the taint of vulgarity and ribaldry that is present in every mediterranean book, is that of dating. Any first book is always in the nature of a tardy settlement of an account with the past, and in this case my debt is with the nineteen-twenties. It was a period when art was concerned with futility, when heroes were called Denis and Nigel and Stephen and had a tortured look. I wonder who remembers them now. In any case I think I may claim to have created a young man as futile as any. It also dates because the life it deals with has almost disappeared; the last lingering colonies of expatriates have now been mopped up, and if you were to pass by Trou-sur-Mer you would find no trace even of any of the characters in the Rock Pool. The bars are closed, the hotel is empty, the nymphs have departed.

There is one more objection I should like to answer. I have been asked why I chose such unpleasant, unimportant and hopeless people to write about, and why I have shown no moral condemnation of their vices. I don't know. I don't know what gives writers their subjects, I know only that in the misadventures of a few people I suddenly saw a story, the myth of Hylas perhaps, the young man flying from the Hercules of modern civilization, bending over the glassy pool of the Hamadryads, and being dragged down to the bottom. And I also saw in it the clash of cultures, the international situation. My hero represents a certain set of English qualities, the last gasp, perhaps, of rentier exhaustion; I felt that in his efforts to adapt himself there was evidence of a predicament which ought to be recorded. As for the moral you must go far back, even to the time when 'the shepherd in Virgil grew at last acquainted with Love, and found him a native of the rocks'.

C.C.

POSTSCRIPT

It is now twelve years since the Rock Pool *was written. The fault of 'dating' of which the author complained has matured into what is almost a virtue, for nothing 'dates' us so much as an ignorance of the horrors in store. And a tidal wave was to engulf the Rock Pool and wipe out all trace of it for seven years. Now, alas, of all those graceful originals from whom the principal characters were drawn hardly any survive. 'Toni' died a year or so after, of consumption, when barely twenty-one; 'Ruby' came also to a tragic end; and 'Sonia', being Jewish, perished in a Nazi extermination camp. Of the two young men from whose worst features the character of Naylor was so competently welded, one has long lost all his arrogance and fire; the other, whose wit, generosity and sweetness, with his extraordinary beauty, had, for purposes of this narrative, to be ruthlessly suppressed, died in the black winter night above Germany. Even the publisher, the charming and faintly mephistophelean Jack Kahane, who waged a lonely guerrilla war against English prudery (and who found my book so little salacious that he used to tell me it was 'a disgrace to his list'), has gone to 'explore the shadow and the dust', and I am appalled to notice how, among the principals, it is only the author and the artist, with their cautious reptilian tenacity of life, who remain. And my old friend – but then he too is an artist – to whom after all these years I am still writing this letter.*

Antibes, 1946.

NAYLOR was deaf again. Nothing serious, a ball of wax in
the ear. He got out of the bus – the vibration hurt him – and
made for the nearest café. It was a town he had never
explored, though he had often passed through it, riding up
and down in the buses from Cannes to Nice – a noisy
modern street to whose tawdriness the setting sun lent a
certain exhilaration, with the old village on a hill beyond.
His ears boomed pleasantly, he heard his own footsteps
very far away, as if he were pacing the corridors of a luxury
hotel, on a rich pile carpet, with the drone of the power
plant dominating the silence. He found a table and sat
down. At first it seemed like other cafés; the zinc, the cash
register, the coffee machine, two lorry drivers playing
draughts; but as he scanned it, his eyes sharpened by deafness, he noticed the remnants of an alien culture. Besides a
few old copies of *L'Illustration*, there were some *New
Yorkers*, all of them of 1929 or 1930, and there was a faded
placard leaning against the wall with 'Boston Baked
Beans'. There were several water-colours, two of tartanes
with red sails entering a sunset harbour, one of an old
fisherman, and one of a donkey going up a cobbled street in
the Clovelly-Assisi manner. The other picture was in oils.
A road fringed by dowdy acacias ran towards a range of low
mountains, the sky was imminent and stormy and nothing moved on the steppe except, bowling along down the
centre, pursued or pursuing, according to your tempera-
ment, an enormous egg. Naylor was fascinated by the
spleen of the colouring, by a sense of impending tragedy
which relieved the monotony of the place: it reminded
him of the elderberries and nettles in the Jewish cemetery

at Prague. We all like obscurity when it is on our own plane: great artists like Epstein and Orpen know how to provide for the public the bewilderment it deserves.

Naylor returned to his table. The waiter put a record on the gramophone. A deep, irritable woman's voice began a song of the late 'twenties, *The Empty Bed Blues*. Suddenly Naylor remembered that this place (how the words dated) had once been an artists' colony. It had been called Montparnasse-by-the-Sea. Now since the slump, since the fall of the pound and the dollar, the deserted town must resemble a buried site, a mound where an archaeologist delves for evidence of a vanished civilization, hoping to find a culture ultramarine and superior to that of the villages of neighbours and contemporaries. Cnossus-sur-Mer! And why not stay here and be the archaeologist? What a thesis! 'American toys and crockery found in a . . .' 'adventures of an excavator in a . . .' 'came the Greeks, Romans, Saracens, Lombards, each brought to the little old hill town something of their . . .' 'last of all came the American artists and what they left, it is the object of this little monograph to point out' – he could be modish and witty and just a little bit learned and tender about it all – like those things about the Romans leaving Britain and Mr Baldwin's joke about the diggers of the future and our disused razor blades. A dead city of the present, that should be his theme, the jungle of the Midi bourgeoisie creeping back on one-time American homes, the plumbing, the central heating going to pot again, the cheap wallpapers replacing healthy paint, *Parlez-moi d'amour* ousting the stricter Blues. He would be the Goethe of a new Pompeii – and, besides, this stuff about the 'twenties was a paying proposition. He picked up another *New Yorker*. It was exactly a week old.

Damn – that spoiled everything – if he hid it perhaps – would it make no difference? He could go on with his excavations just the same – so Crusoe, even, may have stamped upon the print on that unlucky Friday. Now in any case an American must have been there at least that morning. Yet the notion was too good to lose – why not, after all, go on and study the remaining inhabitants in the same way? There were, for that matter, always a few people in the deadest of cities: Les Baux and Petra and old Sarum.

Yes, he must change his role. No longer an archaeologist, but an observer, a naturalist. Such a settlement was as good, easily, as a termites' colony – *The Pond I Know, The Stream I Know, The Artists' Colony I Know*, by Edgar Naylor – aquarium similes were the rage now, in Proust, in Gide, and another in *Point Counterpoint*. Why not *The Rock Pool* – a microcosm cut off from the ocean by the retreating economic tide? An outpost or a blockhouse would have done as well but he preferred the other metaphor.

> Beneath the water, people drowned,
> Yet with another heaven crowned,
> Whom, though they were so plainly seen,
> A film kept off, that stood between.

Naylor was neither very intelligent nor especially likeable, and certainly not very successful, and from the image of looking down knowingly into his Rock Pool, poking it and observing the curious creatures he might stir up, he would derive a pleasant sense of power. Otherwise the only power he got was from his money. He didn't have a great deal, just under a thousand pounds a year over which a trustee mounted guard like a dragon, but he knew how to be handy with it, how to make some people feel he was paying for them, and others, mostly women and artists, that he might be persuaded to. It was the auxiliary motor which enabled him to navigate through life, under a slender canvas of charm and courage, with a certain obstinacy. 'If you have to be lumped, you don't need to be liked', he was fond of saying, and he generally managed to hit back at whoever he was with for something ambitious and stunted in him. His neat appearance emphasized an arrested boyishness in his smooth chestnut good looks. He had pleasant manners which he had learnt at school, while Oxford had fostered, the one through the dons, the other through the undergraduates, two separate veins of pedantry and lechery, which, united when drunk and when sober divided, were the most definite things that you noticed about him. Consequently any intimacies into which he entered never ripened, but were nipped off green by his competitiveness, his delight in catching people out or, worse still, perished in one of his amorous pounces.

Unable to love, however, he still believed, rather pathetically, in disinterested friendship. At the moment he was staying at Juan-les-Pins on a holiday from his work, for he had two jobs, one as a kind of apprentice-partner in a firm of stock-brokers, and the other as self-appointed biographer of Samuel Rogers, the banker-bard of St James's Place. Rogers appealed to him not only because he had lived enormously long, but because in that life (1763–1855) everybody else, from Fox and Beckford to Byron and Tennyson, who had been interesting at the time, had played a part. He knew that from the most accessible biographies of all these he would be able to make up a series of chapters more or less concerning his own hero – and unconsciously he had chosen a man who, besides being easy to fix, and rather coming into fashion, was also, through his snobbery, his great wealth, and a certain niggling smallness of soul, by no means unsympathetic.

As he took another look at the picture which had interested him, a voice said: '*Eh bien, qu'est-ce que vous en pensez?*' He turned round to find a little man with grey hair standing behind him. He was obviously a Jew but his features were so Semitic as to have skipped the more familiar peculiarities of the race and reverted to something Assyrian or Hittite. '*Mais je l'aime, je l'aime,*' he answered with surprised condescension. 'Pretty swell, eh!' went on the Jew. 'Meet Rascasse – a pretty swell painter!'

'My name's Naylor.'

'That's good. English?'

'Yes.'

'Fine. Have a drink. So this is the first time you've been to this lousy hole, Trou-sur-Mer? Gee! That's swell. What made you come here? Are you broke?'

'No, I can't say I am.'

'Everybody's broke here – we've some pretty good people here, fine guys – but mostly they're a lot of bums – you need to be careful; better stick around with me for a little. Eating anywhere? I know a very nice little place up the hill where we can have dinner.'

'No, as a matter of fact I'm not – but you must have dinner with me.'

'Oh, sure.'

Naylor paid for the drinks and they started. The road climbed between drab houses. Elderly peasants and shop-keepers who seemed to have acquired an air of licentious-ness from their customers, watched them from the doors. They panted up through the September dusk, and took a lane which branched away to the edge of the hill and ended in a long flight of steps.

The Bastion Bar was at the top. To the surprise of Naylor it was charming. There was a garden with orange trees and a tank; a pleasant bar with yellow walls and a brick floor; and a room beyond for dancing. They dined outside on the terrace. The food and the local *vin rosé* were good; below them stretched the plain and the dark sea, above them spread an enormous vine whose anthracite clusters pat-terned the leafy ceiling, and whose grapes, served in a great bowl, proved of the delicious *framboise* variety. The bar was kept by two very nice girls, explained Rascasse, one was American and the other English. Their names were Duff and Varna. Rascasse himself came from a Jewish village in Bessarabia. Brought up among hogs and rabbis, his love of painting had conducted him through excessive hardships, from the Bolshevik revolution and the Roumanian annexation to a series of gruelling Paris winters where lack of food and warm clothing had combined with the strain of odd jobs or heavy manual labour in the docks and factories, to turn his hair grey at thirty-one.

Naylor, in return, spoke of the biography he was working on, of his little job in the City, which might one day end in a partnership, and found himself warming to his peculiar listener. To think that the republic of the intellect was so democratic as to set him down at the same small table as this Balkan deserter from a rural ghetto, with his gangster English, his general insolvency! He glowed at the reflection, but before he could express it, they were driven inside by the mosquitoes. Over the coffee he was introduced to the owners. Duff was a tall, blonde, rangy girl, an obvious American, well bred and rather shy, but yet with an air downright and sweeping. Varna was sturdy and dark, with wide-set blue eyes. She had something expectant and glistening about her, like a penguin waiting for a fish. Her voice, when she spoke, was musical yet insistent, with an alarming up-to-date governess quality, the silky voice of a Christian Scientist. As the first specimens to come into his net Naylor found them stimulating. Each wore dark blue sailor trousers and blue and white striped zephyrs; they exuded health and cleanliness, just as their bar did efficiency and order. Being told that they were both English, Naylor and Varna began those elaborate manoeuvres of introduction which are performed so punctiliously in that formal country by its inhabitants and its dogs. Their problem was how to find, while asking the fewest and least indiscreet questions, their common boasting ground. Warily they tackled London, circling over Chelsea and Kensington as likely terrains. Suddenly Varna hazarded the B.B.C. as a potential milling-ground, asked him if he knew a bloke called Haddock, and battle was decorously joined.

'Why, of course I know Bill Haddock.'

'Then you must know Claygate – what fun!'

'Yes, he's one of the directors!'

'Have you ever broadcast, Mr Naylor?'

'No, I've never actually been on the air myself, though most of my friends have.'

'Announcing?'

'No, giving talks mostly!'

'Oh, yes, Alec Waugh has told me all about the talks at the Gargoyle!' (check)

'He's charming, isn't he, though I've always known his brother Evelyn better!' (discovered check)

'I've just missed meeting him.'

'? ? ?' (and wins)

'Well, we must have a chat about Bill Haddock one of these days,' concluded Varna, now in full retreat to the kitchen and leaving Duff behind the bar. Naylor asked her to have a drink with him and they had gin and ginger-ales. Duff spoke little. She had a way of nodding her head with a sage smile and relapsing into moody silence. He noticed little crystals of salt against her fair hair, and that her eyes were rather bloodshot from diving.

'The fairies have stolen our sign again,' she remarked suddenly.

'The fairies?'

'Yes, they've been out to get us since we stopped them dancing together here. At first they came from all over the coast but we had to forbid it, they showed off so; then

Eddie-from-the-top came and tried to make us serve him whisky, so's to get our *petite licence* revoked, but we were tipped off and weren't having any. When they take our board away everybody goes straight on up the street instead of turning off the way you came, and Eddie-from-the-top gets all the custom.'

'If you knew the things we were asked,' continued Varna, who had come back, 'I sometimes wonder if my people would survive if they realized! Why, the French come and ask us for a *petite dame* and a private room, and of course we've absolutely had to give up letting any one have credit.'

She looked at him with meaning. Duff went back to their own sitting-room and began to play patience. Her yellow hair glowed as her head bent under the lamp.

'Of course, it's much worse for Duff, she's the real thing,' went on Varna, lowering her voice as the English do at mention of these sacred subjects. 'The way that child was brought up – yachts, motor cars, her own aeroplane – everything regardless! Why, my own people were very wealthy, you know, but, well, well – I mean!' She broke off into a breathless little giggle and fixed her wide-set green eyes upon him. Naylor suddenly realized that she was middle-class and, worse, was assuming that he was. So she expected him to gape with her at Duff's superior breeding! He decided that she was profoundly antipathetic – that voice like a medium's, those clairvoyant eyes, and that sturdy little body in inappropriate sailor trousers! He smiled back unpleasantly and tried to think of a reply. At that moment the door opened and three women came in. There was a fat lumbering girl in workman's slacks; an elderly creature in a man's tweed suit, with a red handkerchief round her neck, an apache cap, a pipe in her mouth, and the leer of a gin-sodden dockhand; but Naylor stared most at the girl who was between them. She wore a white

Russian blouse with a high collar, and a blue Salzburg jacket. Not tall herself, the brown legs emerging from her blue leather shorts were yet surprisingly long. Her face had an extraordinary sweetness combined with a Mongolian beauty of bone. She had dark hair cut like a boy's and parted at the side, slanting grey eyes, a small nose, a mouth like a crushed blackberry, and minute pointed ears. She wore no make-up, but with her body of an archaic Dorian bronze and her little gipsy face, was the image of one of those dainty and heartless fauns with whom Georgian poets delighted to people the Oxford copses. No wonder Naylor fell madly in love with her. She spoke to no one but began to dance with the apache lady.

> In the something traffic's boom,
> In the silence of my lonely room
> I think of you.

The plaintive disturbing harmony floated out over the vines and the olives: the warm night, on which summer's hold could yet be imagined as faintly relaxing, seemed to wait breathless at the door-way. For Naylor it was one of those miracles which we have a right to when young, but which later on arouse in us only an apprehension of calamity. He knew that, whatever her name or means or station, here was the girl that he would marry; she alone could exorcise the monasticism, the sour thorn-apples that English education had implanted, 'for she my mind hath so displaced . . .' He tried to remember the quotation.

The music stopped and he went over to Rascasse.

'Who is that girl who's just come in?'

'Oh, so you like the look of her, do you? Well, that's little Toni, Toni von Schaan. I'll introduce you, if you like.'

'I'm going to marry her.'

'Swell. She's a dear little kid. She jus' doesn't know what she wants, that's all.'

'She is a friend of yours?'

'Sure. I lived with her.'

'Er – when was that?'

'In the spring.'

'I don't care. I'm going to marry her.'

'Oh, it was quite platonic – Toni's a very platonic little girl.'

'I didn't mean that at all; I simply mean that I should rather like to meet her.'

'Oh, sure, I understand. I'll fix it.' He walked over to her and began talking.

Naylor felt Napoleonic. He folded his arms and leaned back and looked fierce and interesting. He recalled those English milords who romantically married just such gipsy-looking creatures. People would stare and wonder who she was as they entered the Savoy Grill or the Café. He would let her sit to Henry Lamb. In the summer they would canoe down warm rivers and sleep out on the banks; in the winter she would wear little astrakhan jackets and go to cocktail parties. A new life for her! 'How good you are to me,' she would say, 'I didn't know a man could be so kind and good.'

'May I present Mr Naylor', said Rascasse with a grimace. 'Baroness von Schaan.'

Naylor rose and bowed stiffly. Baroness! and he had loved her when he thought she was nobody! He called for a bottle of champagne. His French was sketchy, his accent better, except that he threw all the emphasis on the last syllable and got cross much too quickly if he was not understood. *'Garçon, une bouteille de champagne, s'il vous plaît!'* He tried a few *mais alors, eh bien quoi, j'ai commanDÉ une bouteille* till it arrived and was opened, frothing. The baroness put her hand over her glass and whispered to Rascasse.

'She wants to know if she can have a Cap Corse instead,' he explained.

While Naylor ordered, she got up to dance with the
apache woman, and, after a few turns, sat down at her
original table, where the Cap Corse was brought to her.
Naylor started to flick his fingers and mutter. For the first
time he began to doubt his love.

'She's a sweet little kid,' said Rascasse, 'she's jus' terribly shy.'

'But really, I mean – it's oneoftherudestthingsthat's-
everhappenedtomeinmylife.'

'Oh, that's just Toni. She's scared of you. You ought to
go ask her to dance.'

'I certainly shan't.'

'She doesn't mean anything by it, she feels she oughtn't
to leave her party.'

'Her party!'

'Oh, never mind, I'll fix it.' Rascasse went over and
began dancing with her, while Naylor rotated his glass
earnestly. He didn't look up when they sat down.

'Feeling blue, eh? *T'as le cafard, quoi?*'

Getting too familiar, thought Naylor, but he turned and
asked the baroness if she would like another liqueur.

'Oh thank you so much,' she answered in a low and even
voice with the freshest and purest accent imaginable. He
adored her.

'Is it good?' he ventured.

'Oh, yes, would you like to taste it?' She held the glass
out awkwardly. Her brown arm was covered with golden
hairs; her hand was long and delicate, the close-bitten
nails were very dirty. Beneath the blouse, with its Russian
collar, the small firm breasts seemed made with halves of
broken tennis balls. Think of something to say.

'Why do you drink that stuff, Baroness?'

'Oh, I learnt to drink it in Corsica.'

'When were you there? I know Corsica.'

'This spring.'

'I was at Calvi.'

'Oh, yes, Calvi is very mondain.'

'Where were you?'

'Oh, I was walking, you know. We were mostly at Cap Corse.'

Heavy going.

'You went with a friend?'

'Yes, but he had to go back.'

Now for it.

'You're fond of walking?'

'Oh, yes, very.'

'Come for a walk tomorrow.'

'Yes, if you like.'

'Where shall we go?'

'Shall we say Saint-Pierre?'

'That's about ten kilometres from here,' said Rascasse, 'way up the valley.'

Have to ask him as well.

'All right. We'll meet here and walk up for dinner. You must come too, of course.'

'Swell. I'll be there.'

'Have you seen the dancers of Saint-Pierre?' asked Toni.

'No, I've heard of them. Would you like to go? I'll get tickets.'

They would do to talk about.

'Oh, thank you so much.'

'And I'll book a table at the Roseraie.'

'It's very expensive.'

The darling!

'Never mind that.'

'When are you coming to sit for me, you little devil?' said Rascasse.

'When you ask me.'

The music stopped. They began to turn the lights down. Naylor paid rather a large bill; by an oversight of which he

12

was only dimly aware it contained all the *fines-à-l'eau* of the other occupants of Toni's table. They started down the hill to the bus stop. Toni, her small shoulders held back, went a little ahead; her walk, like everything else about her, was exquisitely free and natural. Naylor contrived to mention to Rascasse that he would be very glad to buy any picture that he did of her, perhaps she would sit for him tomorrow? – in fact, he would commission a portrait. At the main road Toni turned round. 'You must walk back with me to my room, Rascasse – because – because –'

'Because what?'

'Because I am afraid of a ghost there.'

'What kind of ghost?'

'Oh, well – she is a woman with very red hair, very cold, sometimes she is thin and sometimes she is fat. She comes very close and goes away at the same time like a *pendule*. She is the ghost of a mountain in Finland and she wants me to go back because I promised never to leave her.'

The midnight bus from Nice could not have arrived more opportunely.

II

NAYLOR woke late, with a hang-over. It was relatively a new sensation for him, for he was proud of a certain donnish temperance. He would take two whiskies at night and suddenly round on those of his friends who had a third one. Not that he minded, only it seemed rather childish; remember the law of diminishing returns? And why make yourself sick the next day? But strangely enough he was not sick – instead he seemed to be spun up in a kind of voluptuous cocoon. The sun streamed in over the purple bougainvillea. He tottered down to the sea. Lying on his back, the curious sensation was stronger, his stomach seemed made of wool, his throat felt some rich sensual craving, his mind floated among a multitude of associations, all his senses were slowed up to an unusual delicacy. He masticated a line of Eliot: 'The notion of some infinitely tender, infinitely suffering thing'. Opening his eyes, the sky and sand were grey as a photograph, his antennae played over the tiny crystals, women's brown legs passed him on the board-walk, but he could not look up. 'You see in me a creature in the most refined state of intoxication,' he thought, and waves of sensual and lotophagous reminiscence swept over him. He pushed his inert body slowly into the sea, till his back, his legs, and at last his bottom floated clear. There were no waves. The whole of the Juan-les-Pins shallows consisted of scent and oil, to where began, a hundred feet beyond them, the authentic brine. Still pushing with his hands and lying on his back he reached the salt water. Toni von Schaan! It is possible to raise sentimentality to the point of passion and, like the ocean swathing the nape of his floating neck, he felt her beauty envelop him. She absorbed all the day-dreams he had ever enjoyed: as an only child inventing games in suburban gardens, where the rhododendron and fruition-scented privet yearly bloomed; as a schoolboy, where the bare arms of his neighbours lying across uncharted ink-channels had warmed the desks in summer – till now, when the tepid waves broke over the spindle shanks of his figure that owed so much to conservative tailors, and he seemed to concentrate, in this marine reverie, all his experience into recreating her small disturbing face.

To wake up in love; to wake up with a procession of buried feelings, bars of music, forgotten poetry returning like the cavaliers of sixteen-sixty; to surprise the priests of the oldest, falsest religion celebrating their mysteries in the reconsecrated heart! It does not often happen and, for a moment, leaving the water, he was frightened.

At lunch he propped up the *Continental Daily Mail* and behind it let his imagination run wild; even that dismal paper, which contrives to make all news equally unimportant, from wars and revolutions to cricket, British colony garden parties and lists of new arrivals in Riviera hotels, could not affect his elation, and he ran upstairs to his room. There he lay down and tried in vain to go to sleep while the hot afternoon battered on the orange blinds, until the thought of Toni – her cool, fresh voice, her high brown cheeks stained with red, made him groan with anticipation and bite the bolster and the pillow. In a small attaché case beside the bed lay his manuscript, thin bundles of paper neatly clipped together with a typed chapter heading on each: Rogers and Beckford. Rogers and Byron. Rogers and Wordsworth. Rogers and Italy. But if lacuna there were in the proposed biography, it was Rogers and Sex.

Shaved, washed, wearing white flannels and a dark green tie, he was soon on the bus, which seemed to be driven purely under the impetus of his own desire. The hot square of Antibes, the harbour where the Tunis sea-plane glittered, the long flat shingle with the feathery Alps ahead, fled by him; then the Loup was crossed with its cool moment of northern poplars, and he was back in the café of Trou-sur-Mer. Rascasse greeted him noisily.

The shadows lengthened. The saucers began to pile up. 'Well! What can have happened to that kid, eh, Naylor! Hey, don't look so solemn. Maybe she's forgot. I'll go up to her place and fetch her if you like.' Naylor scowled and muttered. He agitated his knee with great rapidity while flicking and twitching his fingers. His sad, solemn face strained over the empty glass. 'It really is intolerable. Perfectly outrageous. It would simply have been common courtesy to have let me know.' He felt a moment of profound misery, a moment when he considered that nobody really cared what happened to him; his idea of himself as a free spirit who observed the prisoners of the world from the right side of the bars turned to a conviction that he was in solitary confinement; that they were watching him. He had enough money to avoid the general discipline of the professions, and not enough to buy more than indifferent consideration. It was absurd – he should be able to purchase enough love to float a house-boat, and yet people, though glad enough to have dinner with him, were never so interested as to ask him back. Too old at twenty-six. Some gland defective, some minute secretion omitted, and the result was a personable human being whom nobody bothered about, and who could not find it in his heart to bother either.

'You know who you look like,' said Rascasse, returning. 'I've been trying to think and now I remember. You look like the Czar. Yes, pretty smart! Nicholas II, Czar of all the Russias.'

'The Czar was never really smart – he never went to Countess Moussey Moussine's.'

'Of course he was smart, he was the Czar, he was like God.'

'Would you consider Him smart, Rascasse?'

'Him – oh, yes – He is the *Clou de la Saison*.'

Sharing their facetiousness each felt suddenly younger and more friendly.

'And what about Toni? – is she smart?'

'She doesn't care – in Italy they jailed her as a tramp, till they found out she was a woman.'

'And did you find her just now?'

'No, but I think maybe she's gone on.'

'Well, let's have another Pernod.'

'O.K.'

The filmy green drink with the fierce clear flavour was already beginning to perform.

'You know, this is the most intellectual booze,' said Rascasse. 'It goes straight to the cerebrarium!'

'I've never had it before.'

'It's a very good friend of mine, but it's the most dangerous drink of all – why, I've seen it kill people, yes, kill them – and all the worst fights start on a Pernod jag.'

'It tastes quite harmless.'

'Well, what do you think – why you can go mad on Pernod – it gives you the quickest kick of any drink, but then it's the first to wear off. There's an American girl with a studio near mine who has it for breakfast.'

'But it's not really bad for you like this, is it?'

'Oh, you've got to be having sixteen or twenty a day before that.'

'Well, it's a damn sight better than Cap Corse.'

'Ah! I can see you've got a tongue, Naylor, we'll have to look out in Trou-sur-Mer.'

'Well, one must get something after four years at Oxford.'

'Still – poor little Toni – she doesn't know much about food and drink – she's pretty glad to get anything.'

'But how does she live?'

'Well, she's been living on oranges for the last three days.'

'But can you allow it?'

'Well, I'm afraid I have to live on oranges myself.'

'Oh, I'm sorry – but really you must let me – here's something on account for the portrait you're going to do of Toni, and here's something to give her for sitting.'

'Oh, thanks a lot. What say we have another drink and go up on the bus, then if she's started walking without us, we'll pass her and pick her up?'

'Splendid, Rascasse. By the way, what's that book?'

'Why, the greatest literary genius of the hemisphere, Walt Whitman, *Leaves of Grass*.'

17

The fiery anis raced through Naylor. 'My dear sir, how perfectly preposterous. You can't say things like that.'

'I can and do. Look what he says, "I resist anything better than my own diversity". That is a profound remark. You would say it was Paul Valéry. "Every condition promulges not only itself, it promulges what grows after and out of itself, and the dark hush promulges as much as any. I open my scuttle at night." '

'Now, Rascasse, a word of advice, stick to painting.'

'Well, that's what I do. I stick to painting.'

'But Whitman . . .'

'Walt Whitman was a very great painter; what he says, what he promulges, is the language of the painter – only he is a word-painter, the greatest word-painter in the . . .'

'But then he must resemble a painter, and there's no painter like him.'

'Yes, there is, he was like Courbet. Courbet painted like Whitman . . .'

Naylor, as is the case with so many well-educated Englishmen, thought art had disappeared down a mysterious tunnel between Velasquez and Whistler and was silent.

'Well, who do you think is the greatest poet?' conciliated Rascasse.

'Rogers, Samuel Rogers.'

'What did he write?'

'He wrote –

"Mine be a cot beside the hill,
    A beehive's hum shall soothe the air,
A willowy brook that turns a mill
    With many a fall shall linger near.

The swallow, oft beneath my thatch,
    Shall twitter from her clay-built nest;
Oft shall the pilgrim lift the latch,
    And share my meal, a welcome guest." '

'And where did he live?'

'In St. James's Place, in London.'

'Was he a friend of Walt Whitman?'

'No, though I suppose he might have read some of his poems.'

'Did he read "Starting from fish-shape Paumanok" or "As I lay with my head in your lap, Camerado"?'

'I don't know. He was very kind to Americans.'

'They are two of my favourites.'

The Pernods ebbed and left Naylor with an acute headache. They had missed the last bus and had to take a taxi. With the four hundred francs (two for himself and two for Toni) that he had given Rascasse, the drinks at the café, the taxi fare and dinner ahead, it looked like being an expensive evening. The car climbed quietly through the warm pines.

' "The Red Aborigines",' continued Rascasse, ' "heaving natural breaths, sounds of rain and winds, calls as of birds and animals in the woods, syllabled to us for names, Okonee, Koosa, Ottawa, Monongahela, Sauk, Natchez, Chatta-hoochee, Kaqueto, Oronoco, Wabash, Miami, Saginaw, Chippewa, Oshkosh, Walla Walla." Do you like it? Did Samuel Rogers like it? Do I speak it properly?'

But Naylor was silent. He had never missed a bus before.

The hill town jutted out from the mountain like a peninsula. The Roseraie, a modern Provencal hotel with a courtyard and lemon-trees, was built on the neck of land that joined them. Beyond was a fountain under some enormous planes, and the gate of Saint-Pierre, whose black old walls disappeared into the night. Toni arrived from the leafy shadows. She wore a white mess jacket and blue trousers. Her dusky little face seemed more beautiful than he could have imagined. She greeted him with great friendliness. 'Well, there you are!' He held her long cold hand a moment and noticed that her brown forearm had the rippling upper

muscle of a boy's. He felt furious and tearful. 'But we
waited over an hour for you down below.'

'Why, you don't mean to say you really did walk up!'

'No, it was too late. We came in a taxi.'

'Oh, yes? I never thought you'd walk it.'

'Was that why you chucked us?'

'Chucked you! Why, here I am.'

'Well, suppose we have some dinner.'

They moved over to the garden. The restraurant was
empty except for some French journalists having a riotous
publicity evening on the house and a sad-faced English
couple who looked as if they were waiting anxiously for
winter. They could have dinner at 40 francs a head – fish,
chicken, and a *soufflé*. Naylor began to argue about the price.
Rascasse looked at the sky and Toni at the other diners.
The proprietor, who was doing very well out of a reputation for being kind to artists, which drew a richer clientele
to come and see them, realized that this trio was neither
one thing nor the other and said that if they found the price
too much, he regretted, he could be of no assistance.

'*C'est absolument monstrueux, Monsieur. Nous par-
tons.*' And Naylor rose majestically and walked out, followed by his guests. Luckily there was a rival restaurant
across the road where they were offered a more reasonable
dinner and where they sat on a terrace drinking the excellent wine of La Gaude.

During the meal he persuaded Toni to talk about herself.
She came from Courland where, in some vague Gotha-
haunted solitude between the Balkans and the Baltic, her
family had once possessed enormous estates. These they
had lost through gambling seventy years ago, though as the
dinner progressed it seemed only yesterday. Her parents
lived in poverty in some German town with her two
brothers, one a dancer in the Munich opera in his spare
time, the eldest a victim of the family pride, with such a

horror of the human race that he had once had to go to bed for three weeks after standing in a queue. She did not get any money from her parents. Her mother was Polish, her father a direct descendant of the Tartar emperor Hulaku. She made a little money out of journalism, writing chiefly travel stories for German papers. As far as he could piece out her recent existence she had spent the winter in a cottage with Rascasse and a young American; then she had been in Corsica with the young American, who had come back suddenly without her; the summer remained to be accounted for, and she had just arrived from Paris on a bicycle a week ago. He asked her if she had ever been to England, and thought of the happiness he would derive from showing her Winchester and Oxford, the Thames, and the Changing of the Guard. He would teach her to spot Regency buildings, and they would work themselves up about the demolition of Carlton House Terrace and Waterloo Bridge.

'Oh, yes, I've been to England. I was in London quite a lot, and then I was in Skye.'

Rascasse was strangely silent while Toni rippled on, her monologue coming in spurts of her exquisite English, and then being interrupted by drawling hesitations of 'Oh . . . well . . . and then . . . why . . .' Only when her housekeeping with Rascasse was touched upon did he grow lively, and he reproached her with ingratitude. 'I did everything for that little kid. She was broke. We let her come and live with us. She wouldn't do any work. She sat under that plane tree all day. When she did get two hundred francs, she never contributed anything. She bought a pistol and fired bullets through the bedroom door at us till the mayor sent for her and confiscated it.' Toni blushed and giggled entrancingly.

'Well, now, Toni, what do you think?' said Rascasse. '*Tu crois tu peux m'aimer?*'

'*Ah, mais, Rascasse, tu sais que je t'adore,*' she answered.

'What about the dancers? Shall we go?'

'Do you mind very much if I do not come?' said Toni. 'You see, I have seen them before. I will wait for you and meet you in the café.'

The others went on alone through the gate of Saint-Pierre and up a black cobbled street with a drain down the middle. The theatre was a low dark room in which stood some very uncomfortable benches and where they had the worst seats right at the back while thirty or forty fashionable people whispered in front of them. It was a rousing performance. The dancers were two women who seemed like nightmares of Duff and Varna. One was blonde and stringy, English, with a tiny mouth from which two large rodent tusks protruded, the English dentition; the other, a heavy, black, repressed-looking creature. They danced to a gramophone on a tiny stage in costumes they had made themselves, occasionally pausing to lecture the audience and pass round a large pot for contributions. You had to drop something in and then write down your name in a book and how much you had given. This was then compared and the total commented on in relation to that of other performances. Naylor put in twenty francs and wrote down fifty.

'*Je n'aime pas faire le détective,*' hissed the English dancer, '*mais quelqu'un a fait une erreur de trente francs. Je repasserai le petit pot bleu à tout le monde pour le rectifier.*' Several hundred more francs were thus secured and the dances went on. They consisted of mimes, of intimate reveries danced by one or other of the girls, who were only occasionally on the stage together. In so far as they had imagination, and knew what it felt like to be Clytemnestra, Piers Gaveston, Gilles de Rais and Satan, they were a success; it was in the technique of communicating their feeling that they showed less experience. Naylor received a general impression of the hard wooden seat, of long waits, and a series of tableaux in which the English girl flapped about in feminine costumes while the other sweated and strained in robes which revealed her huge gleaming thighs and yellow stomach. They combined the 'nineties of Richard le Gallienne with the spirit of Beardsley's Messalina. The last dance was called the *'Baiser du lépreux'* in which a mediaeval queen hands on her fatal illness to the king's mistress. To the morbid redundancies of Ravel's *Boléro* the dark girl, her face appropriately plastered white as snow, hangs over the fainting blonde and imprints the inexorable kiss which, ostensibly her revenge, was obviously for both of them a Freudian labour of love. The audience gasped and muttered: *'L'amour – La Mort – C'est osé!'* while the queen, triumphant, raised her harsh, white face in a fiendish smile which changed to a hysterical chuckle as the curtain came down.

They were delighted to rejoin Toni in the café. This also was a superior place and kept by just such another couple as was the theatre. Naylor was now used to being welcomed by tall, anaemic blondes each with a grim and swarthy protectress. (This one, according to Toni, was no less than Princess Rustchuk.) They ordered expensive little quarter bottles of champagne and soon the bar filled up with the audience and at last with the dancers themselves, who came for congratulations. The English girl was explaining in her amazing accent: *'Oui, la prochaine fois on va danser le Spectre de la Syphilis après Jocasta, et Aucassin et Nicolette au lieu de la Veuve d'Ephèse – ca sera très réussi, n'est-ce pas?'* The brunette sat quietly in her black dress through which Naylor seemed still to see her flat breasts like coolie hats, and her long navel.

'They are very amusing, of course, but you understand

why I didn't want to see them twice,' said Toni. 'What did
you think of them?'

'I do understand,' said Naylor, 'but I don't see in that
case why you made us come all the way up here for
dinner.'

Toni lowered her eyes to her glass and smiled. They had
to take another taxi all the way back and Naylor discovered, by the time he got to bed in Juan-les-Pins, that he
had spent over ten pounds.

III

THE next day he realized how lonely he was. What was his
life in the hotel? He knew nobody. He had chosen Juan-
les-Pins because he liked the heat, because he had been
told that all the pretty women went there, because in
September the rest of the coast was deserted. But he hated
it. The beach, where the fetid waves of sunburn oil lapped
tidelessly on the sand; the board-walk where the hairy
ugliness of the men was so much more noticeable than the
beauty of the women; the hotels and modern shops; the
stream of buses; the casino with its false smartness; the
big cabaret with its curiously plump and vicious Soho
band-leader, all disgusted him. In the streets he seemed to
wade through quarrelsome women in cheap pyjamas. At a
table in Maxim's he noticed a prostitute called Russian
Anna with whom he had occasionally haggled in Piccadilly
attended like an Infanta by five dusky South Americans
with gold lockets bouncing on their chests. In the English
library he found a little consolation and took out several
more volumes of Russian memoirs, for he was a great
armchair snob, and in his reading could seldom find company too high for him. This time he bathed at La Garoupe,
floating on the waters of the wooded cove and looking

across at the remote and snowy Alps beyond. It was his favourite beach: for him the white sand, the pale translucent water, the cicadas' jigging away at their perpetual rumba, the smell of rosemary and cistus, the corrugations of sunshine on the bright Aleppo pines, held the whole classic essence of the Mediterranean. He came back to Juan and sat in the café. Tarts, gigolos, and motorcar salesmen seemed the only public. 'Countess Moussey Moussine in her swell limousine', he recited. No one took any notice of him. It was a world of externals, where jewellery and large cars formed the true background. Naylor felt small and dowdy and realized how very happy he had been the evening before. He recognized in Toni an integrity, a total freedom from that interference, that static of the external world which destroys the harmony of those who do not live entirely in the imagination. And Rascasse! There was a real person – a rugged, honest, single-minded lover of the brush! Both in fact had a vocation, and he recognized unwillingly how deeply that could compensate for the lack of all other possessions.

Now that the dust was laid by evening, he wandered up the road to Antibes, whose austere towers seemed magical in the pearly twilight. He walked between a forest of masts and the forbidding sea-walls, and dined at Basso's, off hot Italian food, by the smells of the harbour. The hulls of large yachts were visible through the arches, his napkin had violet stains, the mosquitoes hummed in the torrid air. Brooding over a bottle of chianti and scratching his shins, he made up his mind to go on up to the Bastion. It was the hour when the soft night of southern cities holds the clearest promise of release and adventure, when a light going on or off is a portent and the lowering of a blind seems like a sign from heaven. He caught a bus to Trou, sweated up the hill, and found the little bar pleasantly illuminated. Varna met him in the door-way. 'Oh, hullo, it's you. This is our gala tonight, you know.' She was busy tying ropes across the garden. 'We have to rope it off on gala nights, otherwise people go out and get up to all sorts of things.' She looked at him complicitly as the matron of a girls' school might at an obstetrician who'd had to be summoned.

'Do they really. How beastly!' he heard himself saying, as he hurried in. The red-tiled dance floor of what had once been the kitchen was crowded. Everybody wore shorts and there were more women than men. Rascasse began to shout at him.

'Well, of all the guys! Why, look who's here.'

Various people whom he had never seen regarded him with animosity. Rascasse introduced him to a girl called Lola with whom he was dancing. She was small, voluptuous, heavily painted. Her hair was golden, she looked up at him and smiled. He found himself dancing with her and ploughing away in her horrible language. '*C'est long*TEMPS *que vous etes ici, mademoi*SELLE?' She shrugged back and made a face.

'*Mais oui.*'

'*Et vous etes heur*EUSE *ici, j'esp*ERE.'

'*Mais non, monsieur, je me suis mortellement ennuyée.*'

'*Mais pourquoi?*'

She shrugged and made another face, rather more drastic.

'*Ah, monsieur, j'ai des chagrins d'amour.*'

Naylor was delighted because, being perfectly a tart, she seemed to him perfectly French. She clung to him while they circled and gave him long, soft *Vie Parisienne* glances. Afterwards they rejoined Rascasse.

'Well, what do you think of her? Isn't she sweet?'

She disappeared to the ladies' room. It transpired she was in love with a young Corsican who worked in Nice and who was terrified of his wife finding out that he slept with her. She had been a model and had been on the cinema. There was a stir at the door. Toni came in. She was even more simply dressed than usual, in a pair of old grey trousers, a coarse white flannel shirt and a red hand-kerchief tied round her neck. She stood in the door for a moment with her hands in her pockets. She held herself so erect that all other women seemed to stoop when one looked at them. Behind her came another girl in white ducks, with a small tanned face beneath ash-blond hair. Their appearance was devastating as they advanced with their arms linked, the dark and the light head, each serious and finely shaped, side by side. They were followed by a man in a kilt, complete with heavy tweed jacket, sporran and skeandhu. He sat down, wiped the sweat off his fore-head and said: 'Well, how about a bottle of wine?' The two girls glanced at each other and soon were sipping the inevi-table Cap Corse. Toni came over to Naylor and shook hands with him; then went back to her party again. Lola returned and had a *verre de Cinzano*. Rascasse explained that the Highlander was called John Foster. He had a villa on the top of the hill and an American wife who was away. He travelled a lot and had a little money. The other girl he had never seen. The Corsican arrived in plus-fours. He was handsome, though getting fat, a rake in harness, and carried Lola off to dance.

'It's no good trying to get that little Toni to sit,' said Rascasse, 'she won't stay still ten minutes – supposing I paint you instead?'

Naylor accepted and felt that he had scored off her. He was shown other celebrities of the town: the terrible Eddie, who kept the rival bar at the top of the hill (a large, fierce American with a mean expression) and his friend Jimmy, who appeared equally tough were it not for an intimate little voice of the 'Vortex' period and a mop of peroxide hair. There was also an unfrocked clergyman who had followed an extremely drunk young woman all the way from Capri. She had large flabby arms covered with piqures and came with a fat ginger-haired girl friend. There were one or two more American painters, tousled, and earnestly drinking, and the same large woman of two nights before in her workman's cap. The gathering did not provide much evidence of human progress, and certainly reminded Naylor that he was on the wrong side of Eden. But still who was he but an investigator, an entomologist, a gaol inspector? After a certain amount of whispering the young man in the kilt came over. 'Good evening,' he said, 'I hear you're English – one doesn't meet very many English people here. My name's Foster. I say, were you at Oxford? I was at Cambridge. What did you do? Did you raow? Did you reide?'

'No – what did you do?'

'Oh, I played paolo.'

Naylor thought for a moment of horses, those fierce, inscrutable creatures always slobbering, urinating, champing their orange tusks and trying to bite him, and decided to change the subject. After all, as the challenged, he had choice of weapons.

'Really? What fun. What college were you at?'

'Sidney Sussex.'

He's on the hop.

'I'm afraid I don't know anyone there – were there any Wykehamists?'

'Nao – were you at Winchester?'

'Yes – where were you?'

Groggy – can't last.

'Berkhamsted.'

'Oh, yes, I've heard of it – it's very healthy, isn't it?'

'More than this place is, don't you think?' said Foster, trying to establish equality on another footing. 'Do you know the Riviera well?'

'No.'

'I lived five years on Cap Ferrat, then I got tired of the social saide and moved up here. I wraite. Are you staying at the Pension Oustric?'

'No – I'm at Juan-les-Pins.' He felt like the second most unpopular boy at a school receiving overtures from the first.

'Quite reight – they're a very worthless lot up here – I'm away most of the time.'

'Where do you go?'

'Oh, I'm very fond of uncivilized places. I like primitive people. I've just come back from Guadeloupe. Do you like primitive people?'

'No, I don't. I like very sophisticated places, with champagne in buckets.' He thought of asking him if he was wearing the old school tartan, but at that moment Foster turned round to see Toni and the blond girl dancing together. The blonde girl was leading and taking long, masculine strides, she was as young and thin and as beautifully built as Toni. They looked like cheetah kittens among a herd of sows. Foster began haranguing them. He seemed very angry. Toni shrugged her shoulders and walked out. A moment after she had gone Foster planked down a fifty-franc note and went after her. The other girl followed. Naylor rose and joined in the chase. He got a not-quite-cricket look from Varna as he went, and a leer of contempt from the apache lady. He found himself in a steep cobbled street that smelt of drains. The blonde girl was beside him. She turned round and smiled. '*Et vous, qui est-ce que vous cherchez?*'

'*Personne – je me promène.*'

She took his arm. He leaned over and kissed her on the cheek. Round the corner they discovered Toni walking down the hill with Foster, his kilt flapping. Naylor asked the other girl a few questions. She was German, her name was Sonia. She had just arrived that evening and was staying with Toni.

'*Ich bin so müde, so müde,*' she sighed and went on in laboured English. 'It is terrible. I get so easily drunk. Let us talk philosophy. What is your philosophy?'

'Opportunism.'

'What is that?'

'Making the most of my chances.'

'Pah – how material.'

'Well, why not?'

'But you are young. Later you can be material – now is the time to believe.'

'But I do believe – I believe in opportunism.'

'How silly – what about life – what is life – what is progress – what is growth?'

'But I do believe in growth and progress. I believe that one is young, then not so young, then old, then very old, then dead; timid, then bold, then cautious, then crusty, then feeble; fresh, then stale; innocent, then guilty, then totally indifferent; first generous and then mean; thin then fat; thoughtless then selfish; hairy then bald – what more can you want?'

'*Ah, vous êtes terrible – vous êtes terrible.* I wish I wasn't a virgin – I feel so silly when you talk like that – but it is so difficult, I can't find the man I like.'

'Then you haven't got a lover?'

'No, of course not – but let us talk philosophy. Do you believe in the first cause?'

He thought of Rogers who used to explain that he was always malicious because his voice was so weak that it would never carry if he said anything kind, and remembered a little of his own passionate adolescent interest in right and wrong. 'I believe there was a first cause who made the world,' he answered, 'but I think it got discouraged too easily.'

This was what she liked, trying to rectify the wandering judgement of her senses, the influence of sex and wine, with logic and mental discipline. The ethical dormitory whisper.

'But if there is a first cause, it must still be operating. *Parlons français. Parce que pendant que les causes secondaires se dérivent, il faut que la cause première existe en eux aussi.*'

Like most Germans, she spoke other languages with a clumsy, passionate accent, but unlike them she possessed a certain crispness of form, her slight figure seemed whittled out of some hard pale wood, her hair was like a mustard field.

'And what virtues do you admire, monsieur?'

'Oh, keeping alive – keeping alive.'

'You do not think suicide beautiful?'

She strode into the bar where he had first met Rascasse and to which they had now descended. Sonia walked straight over to Toni and Foster and joined in the altercation that was still going on between them.

'Listen, Sonia,' said Toni, 'I don't want to talk to you while you're drunk. Afterwards you can get drunk, but tonight you've got to talk to me.' They all began to talk German very fast and Naylor couldn't understand them.

Rascasse, Lola, the Corsican, Eddie-from-the-top, the peroxided Jimmy appeared in succession.

'Here, don't forget this, mon cher, Varna asked me to give it you. She said that any time would do.' It was a bill for seven *fines-à-l'eau*, three packages of cigarettes, and one dinner, and reminded him that he still had a certain position to maintain.

'I suppose they had to give the Trobrianders a good deal of booze before they'd talk,' he said.

Rascasse smiled and give him a long quizzical look. 'I'm just thinking how I'm going to paint you.'

Naylor, still irritated by Varna's bill, felt anxious to be revenged on him, but another urge was uppermost, man's oldest, saddest quest.

'Look here, Rascasse, I don't want to be alone tonight, *ayant peur de mourir lorsque je couche seul*. Now – what about Toni?'

'Not a chance, you've got to go very slowly with her. She's a dear little kid, but she's not quite sure what she wants, and she mustn't be frightened.'

'Well then, Lola?'

'She's a swell girl and she certainly likes you, but lay off while the Corsican's around.'

Naylor felt he could come to the point.

'I've had a great talk with that German girl. She's absolutely sweet. Really quite touching. She's only nineteen.'

'I don't know anything about her, but I should think Foster would be very jealous. You'd have to be very careful.'

'Well, why don't you try and get her away from his table for me?'

'I can't promise anything.'

Rascasse went over and sat down with them. Naylor bought himself a large whisky. Lola sat with her elbows at the bar, her chin in her hands and a straw dangling from her lips. She pouted at the Corsican, staring at him with large empurpled eyes. Eddie and Jimmy were on the other side of her. Suddenly the door opened and a woman ran in with head down and arms folded, as if she was battling with a gale. 'It's only me – it's only little Ruby,' she screamed, and gave the men a playful butt. She had black hair and a remnant of prettiness. She was not wholly unattractive, and seemed accessible even to some one of Naylor's technique. She quickly singled him out. 'Welcome, stranger, what have you got in that glass?' Soon they were walking uphill to her cottage. She was American, a composer. She had the passion of her countrywomen for double meanings and giggled delightedly when she brought one off. She hugged Naylor several times as they rested on the hill and he congratulated himself that he had made the most of what he could get and justified his philosophy, instead of pursuing the unattainable. But the price of wisdom! To lose Toni for this animated little drunken bundle! He stopped for breath again.

'Not cross with little Ruby? Because if you are, she's not going to take it lying down!' She began to giggle again. Then suddenly turned on him. 'What are you doing here – why are you following me – you aren't an artist – you don't understand what we live for – offering me food and drink like that – what do you think I care about food – do you think I'm interested in your beastly money – you've no idea what our art means to people like us – it's nothing to you, just nosing around here because you bore yourself any place else – why don't you hang around the casinos?'

'But you don't understand at all. I like you. I like you a lot.'

'You don't. You hate me – and I hate you – see?'

'Ruby!' She squeezed him again. All was well.

They went through a kind of tunnel between mouldering pensions and reached her house. There was only a studio and a kitchen. She lit a candle, coyly asked him to look the other way, and undressed. When he turned round she was getting into bed. He did not know whether to undress too and decided to wait a little. He sat down on the narrow bed beside her. He felt something stir underneath. A cat perhaps? A tow-coloured head appeared from under the covers. It was a pale undersized child of about eleven – a girl.

'Had a good time, mummy?' But her mother was already snoring. The whole room suddenly reeked of Pernod. He tiptoed out and ran back the way he had come. Rounding a corner he went straight into a bulky figure. It was Jimmy. With his extraordinary peroxide mop he looked like a decaying viking.

'Hey – hey – not so fast – don't be so disconcerting,' he lisped. 'Why, it's you, you charming creature, I was just wondering if I should meet you – don't think you took me in with that he-man role. Not with those long, bisexual ears – Let's go and have a drink at my place.' Naylor struggled to get free but his elbow was held in a grip of iron, which was clearly the result of long practice.

'Let go. Letmegothisinstant.'

'Oh, don't be so difficult. You aren't afraid of an old-fashioned sadist. You don't often meet with them now.'

'It's perfectly monstrous. Let me go.'

'Oh, don't be a firebrand.'

Naylor changed his tactics and tried to purr.

'Look here, I like you tremendously, we must certainly discuss this some time – supposing I come for a drink tomorrow?'

'Well, it is tomorrow now.'

'No, it isn't.' Jimmy held up his wristwatch and pointed to the approaching dawn. Blue stubble ran all the way up his cheeks to his plantinum hair. Naylor darted past and fell flat on the cobbles a few yards beyond. A door opened beside him. It was Rascasse's and he and Jimmy between them carried him in. 'Silly little fool,' Jimmy lisped, and went on up the street.

IV

THIS time he woke up with the real thing. Somebody was tapping his skull as if it were a breakfast egg. When he moved loose flints rattled inside it. His mouth seemed full of corrosive sublimate. He had a breath like an old tyre on a smoking dump. He lay on a wooden bench in a dark, dusty room. There was very little furniture – a table, two wooden chairs, a basin, and a bed. Rascasse was painting by the window on an easel. Naylor closed his eyes, opened them, and was sick. For some time after he lay like a crushed snail on a garden path. Rascasse gave him a towel soaked in water and a tumbler of brandy. The sunbeams danced in the window. The flies whirled above him, he felt their damp suckers on his eyelids whenever they were closed. He was through. He would go home. He thought of the office in the city, the regular hours. 'Hullo, Naylor, had a good holiday?' He thought of the London library, the beginnings of autumn in the parks, the mists, the lights being lit, the curtains drawn for tea.

'I'm leaving tonight.'

'Oh, you feel as bad as that, *mon copain*? Here, just wait and I'll get you some Fernet Branca. Besides, you can't go till I've painted your portrait.' He disappeared and returned with a glass of the black draught that most of us learn to appreciate sooner or later. Naylor was nearly sick again but managed to swallow it.

'How long portait take?'

'Two or three days. Suppose we start the sittings this afternoon?'

'Could finish day after tomorrow?'

'Sure.'

'All right. I'll stay.'

The morning passed in slow recuperation. Rascasse painted in silence. There was a pleasant smell of turpentine. Toni looked in. She seemed pleased to see Naylor. He knew suddenly that he was not in love any more. He was too sick to love, he felt; all he could think of was how long it would take him to get his head safely under his bowler. And then he understood that not only had he received no encouragement, but that he had never for a moment made any impression on Toni; she made him feel as if he wasn't in the room. People do not fall in love unless there is a remote chance of success, and those who do are secretly inviting failure. Impotence or some psychological twist prompts the usual 'hopeless' passion. Health and accessibility meant more to Naylor than beauty and marble indifference. He had simply taken rather a long time to find it out. Feeling now so composed about Toni he found that he got on much better with her. He did not get so cross when she took no notice of him and she also seemed less on her guard. They talked pleasantly for a little, till she left them to go up to Saint-Pierre.

'What can she do up there? She's always going up to Saint-Pierre.'

'Oh, she's a funny kid, she jus' sits around. She told me she's going on to Spain with Sonia pretty soon. Sonia arranged to meet her here and they're going off with a donkey. Gee, that's a sweet child. She's a law student in Munich, a serious little girl.'

They lunched off bread and sardines and some fresh tomatoes. Naylor went to sleep again, and when he woke up felt very much better. He began to pose, sitting upright in the wooden chair and smoking to keep the flies away.

Rascasse sang and whistled as he painted, occasionally addressing himself in French. '*Ah, vous serez un grand peintre, Rascasse, si vous travaillez toujours comme ça. Ce qu'il vous faut, c'est une petite femme sérieuse – une jolie blonde.*'

Later on Lola came in. Naylor began to notice how Rascasse's attitude altered with every one he addressed; so far from being rugged and uncouth (the impression which his talkie-American and Aztec appearance first made) he was in reality as fluid as a barman. He was good fellow, serious artist, thinker, and courtier, according to the company. To women he paid elaborate compliments and

made protestations of affection. Lola enjoyed these particularly and looked as if she were going to sing a song about
les filles petites du quartier at any moment. She had a
mouth of extreme sensuality, and a constant histrionic air
of boredom and grief. They all went down to the café.
Naylor began to grasp the rhythm of existence in Trou.
People met and talked a certain amount in the morning
and afternoon, but they were mere ghosts of themselves,
ragged anatomies; at about six they began to come alive,
using the lower town for this purpose. By dinner-time they
were more or less their real selves, like small boats floating
off the mud with the evening tide. After a dinner which
varied according to their means, but which they often all
took together, for seven or eight francs, at some long table,
they tended to gather at the Bastion, except for Jimmy and
the unfrocked priest, who remained faithful shock troops
at the male American headquarters: *chez* Eddie-from-the-
top.

As they walked down the steep road they passed Duff
and Varna coming up from a bathe. Both looked fresh and
clean as Arden girls and gave them but the curtest of nods.
The bar was empty, squalid as only a theatre of human
emotion can be when the element is absent which gives it
life. After a few drinks Naylor seemed better. The platinum Jimmy came in and asked how he felt. Nobody else
had been nice to him for his own sake, even if the motives
were open to suspicion, and he was grateful for once not
having had to make the running. Jimmy was quiet and
sympathetic. There was a great deal to be said for his type,
the oldfashioned Taormina young men. They had their
roots in the past, and were naturally social and cultured.
The tradition of Oscar was still preserved. They were the
heirs of the dandies and inherited his metallic wit. They
tended to be amusing and well-read rather than ignorant
and sulky – perhaps because they pleased and enjoyed

pleasing polite dowagers, while no one had ever heard of their female counterpart gravitating to wordly old men. Naylor gathered from Jimmy that the sex war raged in Trou, and indeed all the way up the valley to Saint-Pierre. The quiet water of the Rock Pool was continually being disturbed by these obscure conflicts, the Amazons fighting in pairs like a female Theban legion, attacking all the men who were attracted to any of the weaker sisters, while the male couples formed the armchair die-hards and fire-eaters on the opposing side.

Jimmy was fascinated by Oxford. Think of it! An Oxford boy! He asked many questions in his Buffalo *Bœuf-sur-le-toit* accent, and Naylor tried to convey something of the gloom, the boredom of college halls and sitting-rooms, the Sunday luncheons, the plates of anchovy toast in the fender, the quiet afternoons spent in running up bills in shops, which formed his only exercise, the autumn evenings with their interminable church bells and fallen leaves. Against these stood out moments of vitality, the rude scholarly jokes, the princely entertainment, life rushing by outside with its murmur of careers and appointment-boards, while within the frowning walls of the medina all was intrigue and languor.

They talked about literature. Jimmy thought the two greatest modern writers were Firbank and Hemingway. Naylor proposed Norman Douglas, Eliot and Joyce. Jimmy praised *Jurgen* and *The Great Gatsby*, neither of which Naylor had heard of. Jimmy knew Gertrude Stein well, and Cocteau and Glenway Wescott, for he belonged to the charmingly dated Paris of the Select and the Bal Musette, and parties on the Ile Saint-Louis, having long been decoyed there from some ferocious small town by the *douceur de vivre*.

Naylor in return told Jimmy about his book – not the life of Rogers – but an earlier effort which the lyricism of his hang-over resuscitated, and the genii imprisoned in the bottle brought magically near. The idea had come to him in the mews and over a garage in one of those refined Mayfair interiors, whose silk cushions and green sofas, with their snoring pekinese in a basket, and their telephones in crinolines Sex the leveller had led him too frequently to explore. The book was to have been an original, racy English picaresque novel, a mixture of Petronius, Harriette Wilson and *Lazarillo de Tormés*. A crisp astringent picture of English harlotry, nearly all dialogue, some of it in rhyming slang and Soho English, the rest in the genteel demotic speech of furnished flatlets off the Tottenham Court Road. For some months it had taken shape in his mind, not as so many printed pages but as something solid and almost edible, a truffle, a garbure, a satura of city life, succulent, expert, with a tang to it, perfectly contemporary: newspapers blowing along the streets in grimy dawns, barrel organs in peeling squares, the expectancy of Charlotte Street, the decay of still-born Pimlico, the hoardings and cafeterias, the noise of shunting; they would live for his readers like the Roman Suburra of Juvenal and Martial – *dum tu, forsitan, inquietus erras* – yes, an unquiet book which people would have to put down in the middle, compelled to slip out into the streets on some sudden, inexplicable, pardine sally.

Why hadn't he written it? Partly because he found he could only write in one language, the dialect of Pater, Proust, and Henry James, the style that is common to mandarin academic circles given over to clique life and introspection. This dead literary English, with its long sentences, elaborate similes and clever epithets effectually blocked any approach to a new vernacular. In addition a heavy vein of Yellow Book preciousness appeared; he became not quite himself when he wrote, as if he had donned the elaborate uniform of a dining-club, and when finally he had disentangled these hairs from his pen, it was to find the competent intellectual vulgarity of Aldous Huxley presiding instead. And after all – why should he write it? It is part of the happiness of youth that the sense of power, like the mystical apprehension of goodness, can be enjoyed to the full without the necessity of projecting it into the tainted realm of action. As with those public-school men who advertise in the newspapers: 'Go any-where. Do anything,' the formula does justice for both will and deed. This conviction of intense disponibilitè is known as promise and whom the gods wish to destroy they first call promising.

'Oh. Ah. Yes.'

Jimmy did not pay much attention to the spurts and silences of Naylor's explanation. It appeared he too was writing a book. 'Just a sensible little thing about myself. It's called *Ah, me! The Mallows!* I think you'll like it. It begins: "There are only two poisons: success and failure. I prefer the alkaline".' He tittered expectantly. Evidently the book had begun like that before. He ended by asking Naylor to tea the next day, at Eddie's-from-the-top. 'I see you're a boy after my own heart, effete, noctambulous, perfervid. After tea you will come and see my books – all the literature of detumescence, and who knows, we may have supper in some delicious night-box!'

He slunk away leaving Naylor mesmerized by his huge shoulders, dyed hair and painted eyes, and the little suety voice that emerged from his great diaphragm.

By accepting Jimmy's invitation Naylor was reminded of his own duty as host and gave Rascasse and Lola dinner in the garden. She seemed grateful for it, though, at times, as he floundered away in his laborious French, he wanted to pick up a plate and break it on her head. It was rather cold in the garden, some twigs had fallen on the cloth and there was a faint mist. The buses rattled past much too close. There were three or four tables under the mulberry trees, with shaded lights on them. Only one other by a bush in the corner was occupied. Foster and Sonia were sitting at it. He was not wearing a kilt any more and they were still arguing quietly in German. As they left Naylor called out 'Good evening' to her. She gave him a perfectly blank look and spoke to Foster. 'Miss Roth is afraid that you must have mistaken her for someone,' he said. She smiled at Rascasse and they disappeared up the hill. Naylor was miserable. The principle of polite society, that unknown here; people appeared to grudge one of causing pleasure and avoiding pain, seemed second's agreeable intercourse and atone for it with unremitting rudeness. Thank heavens he was leaving. He asked Rascasse and Lola for a farewell supper the next night in Nice, and told them to get hold of Toni. The day after tomorrow he would have a last sitting and take the evening train. He caught a bus soon after dinner and once more trundled home through the cistus-scented night.

He slept till lunch-time and awoke perfectly refreshed. The hotel people looked at him suspiciously. His bill had fallen due the day before and they had wondered if he was going to come back. There were a few tiresome letters for him – bills which he dropped into the basket unopened, an inquiry from his private school to know if he had any remarkable achievements, births, or marriages to chronicle in the magazine, and a very unpleasant letter from his bank. England didn't seem such a delightful place to return to after all. He thought of the scabby winter landscape that the close heaven seemed to cover; thin soup under a greasy tureen. And the unreality of it! Even Juan-les-Pins seemed non-existent after the mysterious jungle atmosphere of Trou-sur-Mer; people there seemed to live an intense nocturnal secretive life, to be as shy of observation as an Indian reserve near a densely populated city. It wore the

tragic beauty of those communities which cannot survive
in the world, people there were like the Samoyeds or Mar-
quesas Islanders who simply ceased to breed after associat-
ing with Western man. They resembled the Chleuhs of the
Atlas, wild, gloomy, freedom-loving tribesmen whom the
French hemmed in and starved into surrender. Theirs was
the Bled Siba, the *pays de dissidence* where the hopelessness of the struggle was admitted with fatalism, yet where
all fought on.

He took his coffee at a bar on the beach. The women
were better dressed and better made up than those of Trou,
but not as fierce or as natural. They were as different as the
harem-fed beauties of a Turkish pasha from the gun-
running Macedonian girls of the Pirin. Some, however,
were most attractive. He especially noticed one sitting at a
table with four men, who were of the type that must turn
one or two people into Communists almost every time
they open their mouths. A scarlet Bugatti was drawn up
beside them. Yes, she was remarkable to look at, her chestnut curls waved as she talked, she had a figure like a king's
mistress – not boyish like Toni and Sonia, but broad-
shouldered, with large, firm, pointed breasts, a narrow
waist, flat stomach, and sturdy arms and legs. She wore a
shirt and heavy white canvas shorts on one side of which
there was a large mud-patch. She laughed incessantly,
revealing even, white teeth. It was not possible to imagine
a more splendid human animal. She seemed created as the
last word in specialization for one purpose only.

Not for me, he thought, *non nobis, domine.*

Forcing his thoughts away, he took pencil and paper and
began to arrange problems which, as the observer of the
Rock Pool, he must concentrate on solving.

1. How do Toni, Ruby, Lola actually exist? Where do
they get their money from?

2. Why does Mr Foster wear a kilt?

3. Where is Mrs Foster?

4. Why does Toni always go up to Saint-Pierre? What did she do while he and Rascasse were at the dancers?

5. What was she doing in Skye?

6. Is Foster in love with Sonia?

7. How did Rascasse live till he met me?

8. What was the reason that Toni did not sit for him after I gave him a sitting fee for her – as well as an advance for himself? If Toni has received the sitting fee, why hasn't she thanked me? If Rascasse has kept it, should I ask for it back?

It was not going to be easy to find out, for the natives of Trou only smiled when such questions were put to them. If he could just find someone who would help him, who would confide in him as if he were one of themselves and be less on the defensive! The only people who worked for their living were Duff and Varna. Perhaps they could be of use.

He arrived for the sitting feeling really well. Rascasse drew in the outlines of the portrait and started to paint. It was an afternoon of wind and cloud, and Rascasse began to sing in Russian. His favourite tune was the barbaric melody of the Tartar maidens in *Prince Igor*. As the wild, exhilarating cadence filled the room, Naylor, fighting the flies around his uncomfortable wooden seat, watching his friend engaged on the happiest of all human occupations, felt a sudden uncontrollable ecstasy. He saw the motes dancing in the dusty room and through the open window the deep, invigorating cloud shadows ride over the spurs of the Maritime Alps and scud beyond them across the smoky sea. He remembered a verse from some tiresome saying-lesson:

Happy the man – and happy he alone –
  He who can call today his own,

He who secure within can say:
Tomorrow, do thy worst, for I have lived today;
  Be fair or foul or rain or shine,
The joys I have possessed in spite of Fate are mine.
  Not Heaven itself upon the Past has power,
But what has been, has been, and I have had my hour.

'I'll tell you something,' said Rascasse, 'why don't you stay on a couple of days while it's weather like this and when the picture's finished we'll walk up to La Gaude. I'm sick of all these bums here and they've got a little café there with the best wine in the Var.' He pointed with his brush out of the window to a village that lay about ten miles away on the brown autumnal slopes, where tawny precipices of the Baon descended to the pine woods and were terraced out for vine and olive.

Why go back when there were things like that to do, when he suddenly felt happy and real? He walked about the room to stretch himself and noticed on the mantelpiece a tiny little picture on wood. It was the head and shoulders of Sonia. 'That's lovely,' he said.

'Yes, she's a sweet little kid. She came round here this morning. She's a virgin, she tells me, and only nineteen – the same age as Toni. She walked here all the way from Munich.'

'She walked!'

'Well, hiked, or whatever you call it.'

'Is Foster in love with her?'

'No, no – he's in love with Toni. I had a long talk with him today.'

'Did he say anything about me?'

'He said you were a terrible snob, my friend; he didn't know English people like you existed any more, he hadn't seen one for so long.'

'Why does he wear a kilt?'

'He doesn't as a rule. Toni asked him to put it on that

night – the Fosters are a very old Scottish family. I should have thought you would have known that.'

'Where's his wife?'

'She's somewhere in Italy.'

'What does he do?'

'He's writing a book, I believe. He's a very decent fellow, he's a good guy, a real gentleman anglais, you ought to go and see him.'

'Where does he live?'

'In the villa on the square at the top of the hill opposite Eddie's bar.'

While Naylor was still smarting, Toni wandered in. She admired the portrait and sat down. 'When are you going to Spain?' he asked.

'To Spain?'

'Yes, aren't you and Sonia going to Spain with a donkey?'

'Oh, yes, of course – only I'm not quite sure. Maybe I go to Borneo and maybe I stay here.'

'What does it depend on?'

'Oo-ah-a-ha! It depends on this afternoon.'

'What are you doing this afternoon?'

'Nothing. I thought I'd walk up to Saint-Pierre.'

'Well, I want you to have dinner in Nice this evening with Rascasse and Lola.'

'Oh I should love to, but I must look after Sonia.'

'I'd ask you to bring her – only she cut me yesterday after having a long talk with me the evening before.'

'Oh, but she was so tired that evening – and she never remembers anyone she meets when she's drunk. I'm sure she'd love to come.'

'All right, ask her then. We'll meet at the café down below around seven.'

Rascasse went on painting while Toni told a long, meandering story about her experiences in Ragusa: she was sixteen at the time and had taken command of a band of village boys; they used to swim out at night with knives in their mouths, and steal from the fishing smacks. The afternoon wore on to her pleasant fresh voice, and Rascasse's occasional outbursts of song and self-criticism.

Naylor was in a balmy mood. Like secretly sentimental and poetic people he had a tendency to idealize the company he was in by dramatizing them as the most perfectly representative of their type. It was the glamour of professionalism, the romance of vocation. 'Here am I – take me or leave me,' they seemed to say. 'This is my life. How do you like it?'

With the silvery heave of a dolphin out of the water, the force, the beauty of the present moment seemed to flash into something almost visible and then sink back into the natural current of the afternoon.

The towns of Central Europe where Toni had wandered resounded through her anecdotes – Bologna, Rimini, Zürich, Trieste, Budapest, Prague, Dresden, Warsaw, Riga, Petsamo, Rovaniemi. Over these last Lapland villages she lingered a little and then branched off into Gaelic anecdotes of the Hebrides.

'What were you doing in Skye? When did you go there?'

'Last summer – I went there for my paper.'

'Did you write anything about it?'

'Well, no, not exactly – not yet.'

'Did they pay you to go there?'

'Oh, yes – I had fifty pounds to write a book about England.'

'Did you go anywhere else?'

'Only London.'

'Weren't they rather cross?'

'Oh, yes, I suppose so.'

'Where did you go in London?'

'I went to a café called The Circle – a horrible place.'

'Why on earth did you go there?'

'Well, I didn't know where else to go.'

'Maybe she was broke,' said Rascasse.

She walked over to the door and disappeared. Lola and the Corsican came in. They were an admirable study in vulgarity. Her brand was feminine, his perfectly that of the *jeune homme sportif*. He belonged less to Trou than anyone and began to tease Rascasse. He and Lola between them released more stupidities to the moment than could be imagined. Words like *'moche'*, *'rigolo'*, *'impayable'* fell from them; phrases like *'ah, la barbe!'*, *'quelle drôle de compliment'*, *'votre truc'*, *'votre machin'*. With loving *'oh la la's'* she spat on her tiny rouge-stained handkerchief and wiped and polished his swarthy nose like an old brass.

Naylor left them discussing politics. It was the hour to have tea with Jimmy and for the first time he made his way to the top of the hill. At the summit stood the church, and an old castle of the Grimaldi, and across a little square with an amazing view, Eddie's bar and Foster's villa. Toni and Sonia lived somewhere in the labyrinth of streets below. There was no sign of Jimmy. The bar, which was extremely expensive, and famous for the dilution of its drinks, provided a ten-franc tea of biscuits, marmalade, and a warm, black liquid. He heard the unfrocked priest talking to the woman for whom he had given up so much and gathered there had been some kind of fight. Either Eddie and Jimmy had been beaten up in Nice – one version, or Eddie had called Jimmy a fairy and Jimmy had thrown his drink in his face, or in some women's face. It was either a very spirited or an effeminate action. On the flat roof of his villa, screened by orange trees and palms, he could see Foster strolling with Sonia and with a little man who was bouncing up and down and talking. He walked down by an outside path to the café. He passed a stream that fell down the hill through a grove of giant bamboos. In the cloudy evening the feathery reeds were sad and unsubstantial as a

Chinese poem. 'I am Edgar Naylor, Edgar Naylor, Edgar Naylor,' he thought, 'whose life of Rogers is one of the most amusing, one of the most penetrating, one of the slightest, deepest, gravest, gayest, historically accurate, moving, judicious, imaginative, distinguished, wickedest little trifles, little tomes, that have ever, that has ever come the way of the present reviewer, that it has ever been our lot to award the prize to, to which it has ever been our very welcome duty to award the prize.' And here he was, with his life in his hands, among people, and in places where no Wykehamist, no New Collegeman, no stock-broker, no Naylor had ever previously trod. John Spedding, in his chambers in Gray's Inn, George Bowler, in Gracechurch Street, young Kerr in the Dean's rooms on the front quad, how would they get on in Trou-sur-Mer? Already he felt older and wiser, in a position to patronize them. The discipline of Winchester, that polite and rigorous self-effacement – the best-dressed man is the man whose dress perfectly escapes notice. . . . Other schools may produce more cabinet ministers, but it is the permanent heads of departments, the civil servants who do the work – gradually he felt the crust of it breaking, the weight of manners and tradition giving way, the disapproval, so tactfully voiced, of ushers, parents, friends and tutors counting for what it was worth, and a new, unembittered, impulsive and terrible Naylor free at last. To hell with Rogers. 'Time somebody did something about him! I think you've chosen a very interesting subject! You've got hold of something there. You might look at Greville, and the MSS. in the Record Office.' And again, I might not. 'Good subject' – that wretched old scarecrow! – a man who was always Old Rogers. Unlike Beckford, Wordsworth, Gladstone, or Tennyson, the Young Rogers had never existed; a dreary old eunuch. The albatross fell from him. That night he proposed to get very drunk indeed.

In the café they were waiting. Toni began with a little set speech. 'Sonia is very sorry. She is afraid she cannot come. You see, she has never been introduced to you, and she thinks she ought to stay with John Foster.'

'Thank you. I quite understand. Shall we go?'

They caught a bus and soon were bowling along the Promenade des Anglais past rows of empty boarding-houses. It was customary, in the circles in which Naylor moved, or used to move, to disapprove of Nice – such a horrible trippery place, like Brighton; but he realized that evening how delightful it was; the pink Italian piazzas, the derelict casinos, the Russian churches, the Gothic taverns, the *déclassé* yacht harbour, the musical-comedy palms, the little sea-food restaurants along the front, the Genoese atmosphere of the old town. It was all charmingly dowdy and romantic, like Offenbach, with the aromatic vulgarity of the 'seventies and 'eighties everywhere still in bloom.

Rascasse took them to a crowded restaurant in the Italian quarter. It was what the guide-books describe as *à la bonne franquette*. The food was exotic and delicious, the heat terrible, the waiters impertinent and the large crowd inclined to shout provoking questions at Lola and Toni. Rascasse told them about Nice. The cost of living was lower there than anywhere in France. You could get better vegetables, fruit, meat and fish in the market than any-where else in the south. The wines were excellent and the German restaurants were as good as the French. The people were very tough and it never paid to get into fights with them. Jimmy and Eddie-from-the-top had been nearly killed because Jimmy called someone a fairy. A woman had thrown acid in his face. He went on, as the perfumed Bellay circulated, to describe atrocities in Russia; as a boy he had been to see the execution of three bandits by the Bolsheviks; one had tried to laugh it off and had lit a cigarette and advanced to the firing squad twitching it in the corner of his mouth and giggling. Rascasse had stood out of range with his sketch-book, drawing them till all was over, like a young Leonardo. He described the news of the success of the revolution reaching his distant province, and the old Jews entering the governor's palace, fingering the brocades and curtains, calculating the price of the rich fabrics they had never seen before, and turning the furniture upside down. In one war against the Whites he had fought in the trenches in a platoon commanded by a girl of seventeen, a year older than himself. After the fighting he used to sleep with her. Toni was rather contemptuous and showed them her signet ring with a crescent on it, a bequest from some Mongol ancestor in the Golden Horde. Lola smiled tragically and held Naylor's hand. Our sorrows of the present are more real, she seemed to say, and no suffering can equal a *chagrin d'amour*.

They had some brandy in the arcades. It was a pleasure once more to be in a big city. The crowds, the trams, the cinemas and kiosks would be the same in winter and summer; the alleys under the planes would remain popular when the promenades of Cannes, the board-walks of Juan were unfashionable and deserted. Marseilles was too provincial, too dusty in summer, while in winter the broad Cannebière seemed put there to ventilate the city with the icy north wind. Toulon was charming, but there was no good restaurant, cinema, or hotel, and nowhere to go in the evening but the red-light quarter. Cannes was a fringe of evanescent luxury but not a town. Nowhere in the Mediterranean did the weather of the south and the comfort of the north – sun and butter – unite as here. Besides, there were no writers. All along the coast from Huxley Point and Castle Wharton to Cape Maugham little colonies or angry giants had settled themselves: there were Campbell in Martigues, Aldington at Le Lavandou, anyone who could hold a pen in Saint Tropez, Arlen in Cannes, and beyond, Monte Carlo and the Oppenheim country. He would carry on at Nice and fill the vacant stall of Frank Harris.

'Let's go to Maxim's', suggested Rascasse. They walked towards it under the arcades, rather flushed with brandy; Naylor was with Lola. It had got to be done; the machinery, obsolete, cumbrous, rusty, by which one got into somebody's bed for a few minutes had to be brought into use again, the noisy gears had to be engaged.

'*Lola, comme vous êtes belle ce soir, j'aimerais tellement coucher avec vous.*'

'*Oh, la la!*'

'*Alors ce soir? Vous permettez? Quand on est jeune il faut coucher avec tout le monde, vous savez!*'

'*Ah non, pas tout le monde.*'

'*Mais je vous aime, vous êtes si jolie, puis-je espérer?*'

'*Mais qu'est-ce que c'est la vie sans l'espoir, monsieur?*'

'*Mais cette nuit, vous vous donnerez, s'il vous plaît.*'

'*Alors, c'est entendu.*'

What a charming surrender! He looked down at her young eager painted face, so tenderly cynical, and felt a warm affection for it.

'*Vous êtes une bonne fille, Lola, je te remercie beaucoup.*'

Toni saw them, their arms round each other, and drew Naylor away.

'Well, is she going to make you happy?'

'Congratulate me, Toni. Yes, tonight.'

Her face suddenly contracted. It looked almost black. He thought he had never seen anything so evil. She looked like a wizened monkey. He felt pleased – could it be she was rather more than a little jealous of Lola? She might think she had treated him rather badly perhaps, when she saw that he knew how to console himself. Besides, it would mean dinners and little presents for Lola, and Toni

didn't get very many of them. He would go through with
Lola tonight and perhaps have the other eating out of his
hand in the morning. That was the way to manage women.
Use them, throw them over, play on their horror of losing
anything they thought belonged to them – pay out the
whole sex for the humiliations he had suffered. He strode
through the door of Maxim's at the head of his guests.

It was an urban cabaret. While at Juan-les-Pins the
women wore shorts and pyjamas, dancing in the velvety
night under the palms, here they wore last year's evening
dresses. It was stifling inside; shabbier and sadder than
Maxim's in Paris, lacking the pomp and magnificence of
Maxim's in Lisbon, but exactly right for Nice. He ordered
double whiskies with lumps of ice in them and a Cap
Corse. Before he could take the floor an officer in Spahi
uniform walked up and carried off Lola. He kept her for
three dances running at his table. Naylor was in despair.
Toni refused to dance. Rascasse began to bandy his cheap
compliments with a lady at the next table.

'*Je vous assure, madame, que vous avez l'accent parfaitement parisien,*' Naylor heard him saying, and plunged
into the drink he had ordered.

At last Lola returned. The music began again. Now was
his chance. His face began to twitch a little. He rose and
buttoned his coat. Toni got up too. 'Shall we dance?' she
said to Lola, and before he could speak they were circling
round the room. Toni danced extremely badly, only walking at a slower rate than usual and pushing Lola in front of
her, but he saw her whispering excitedly as they passed
and re-passed. The men at another table began to comment
on her trousers: '*Qu'est-ce que c'est, un homme, une
femme?*' etc. Rascasse looked round.

'Well, feeling blue, *mon vieux*. I guess you're sorry at
going back to England. Why not put it off?' Naylor began to
gibber.

'Going first thing in the morning – gross bad manners –
they never remember for a moment that they are my
guests.'

'Why, what's the matter?'

He pointed. 'She won't let me dance with Lola.'

'Well, let's assert ouselves. You dance with me.'

'Fine, that'll teach them.'

It seemed an excellent idea. They started off, Rascasse
winking and nodding at everyone, Naylor fox-trotting
with gloomy seriousness. Almost immediately the music
stopped. The first saxophone addressed the room: *'Je
défends instamment à ces deux messieurs de danser
ensemble.'*

They stood still uncertainly.

'Merci, quand ils sont assis je peux recommencer.'

Rascasse tried to explain pleasantly. There was a chorus
of *'Sales tapettes – sales Américains – à la rue, à la rue!'*
and a burst of applause when they sat down. Rascasse
joined in it and clapped his hands loudly. To Naylor the
little man stamping and shouting, with a clutch of angry
faces around him, was the most humiliating thing he had
seen.

Toni and Lola came up. 'Well, good-bye, and thank you
for a very charming evening.' They got their coats and
walked out. An elderly Russian in a tail-coat took the floor
and began something stirring and patriotic. Naylor gaped
and muttered. Failure. Not to be liked. Nobody liked him,
nobody wanted him, his presence turned ordinary conversation into whispered asides; in London it was worse,
always parties, 'Are you going to the Bickertons? – Why
didn't you go the Bickertons? – So-and-so meant to ask you
but he didn't know how to get your address.' Perhaps he
smelt. There was something about him that reminded
people of the chasms and abysses of life, his grave uncertain face, his air of wondering if they remembered him,

which he would consciously correct by a sudden aggressiveness. He would go to America and begin life again, surrounded by débutantes and gullible old ladies. 'Dooge, dooge, dushka Oscar poposhka,' sang the choleric Russian. The violins whined, coloured lights revolved on mauve faces. Failure – not to be liked – why struggle, there were places for him. There were the shrubberies of variegated laurel, their dark stems bespattered with starling droppings. There were the tops of wooden pews on which the nose could rest, afternoon sun through stained-glass windows, 'All we like sheep have gone astray; we have turned everyone to our own way'; there were beds in the country, wallpaper and a log fire warming his pyjamas, his mother's kiss when she used to come and say goodnight after dinner, smelling of coffee and chocolates; there was every brand of emotional burrow. He remembered a hot summer afternoon at his private school watching cricket. He had felt a sudden attack of colic, first walking, then running through the long meadow and among tall stalks of sorrel till he reached the school and the cool lavatories just in time.

'Don't get blue because they're gone. Suppose we go to a "house"? There're some pretty good ones round here. We could see a cinema.'

'Why should they go? Why should they leave us like that?'

'Do you miss them so much?'

'Yes.'

'Well, maybe they haven't gone so far. What time is it?'

'Half-past twelve.'

'Well, the last bus will have left. I guess we'll have them back again pretty soon. Sure you wouldn't like to go to a "house"?'

'No, thank you.'

He paid the bill and they walked out into the square.

Toni and Lola were sitting on a bench. 'It's so much cooler out here,' said Toni, 'we thought we'd wait for you.'

There was nothing to say, and after the usual bargaining with the taxis, they departed. When they reached Trou he said good-night to them, called Lola back as if to apologize for something, shoved her into the taxi and drove on. He saw Rascasse waving and Toni scowling after him.

Lola smiled. '*Tiens, un rapt,*' she said.

He nodded grimly. '*Où habitez-vous?*'

'*Mais tout près – à côté.*'

He told the taxi to wait and they got out. He marched her a few yards down an alley and she let him into her modest room. So far he had not seen an interior in Trou which boasted either electricity, gas, or running water, or in fact any other system of plumbing. He decided that was to be another heading in his investigations. For the rest it was soon over. She had been absolutely passive. Her breasts were not too good, and her blonde hair was even more artificial than he had supposed. She insisted that he should leave immediately. He went out into the lane. There was a grass bank fairly close with a large aloe growing on it. He climbed up and fell asleep. When he awoke the sun was shining. His morning headache was as bad as usual. Outside Lola's door he saw the Corsican getting into his Citroën. He remembered that Rascasse had said that he visited Lola every morning on his way to his office at Nice and that his wife was pleased with him getting up so early to work. The corruption of the little town seemed suddenly oppressive.

He walked into the main street. His taxi was still parked by the side. The driver was huddled over the wheel. He went up on tiptoe and peered at the meter. Two hundred and seven francs. There was no sound but the driver's breathing and the tick of the machine, like an invisible auctioneer. Two hundred and seven francs fifty. Two hundred and eight. He ran down a path on the opposite side, through a glade of poplars, away from the tram-lines, beside a stagnant stream. After crossing several main roads he reached the sea. The beach of Trou was a desolate stretch of shingle ending in the swampy delta of the Var. It was barren and uncomfortable, but after the scented boards of Juan, there was something severe and bracing about the line of white pebbles, the calm expanse of open sea. Naylor went back to sleep in a clump of rushes.

V

THIS time he did not wake till the early afternoon. He was alone in a waste of sea and stones, in the grey sunshine. Far out he noticed a swimmer making for land. It was Toni weaving a slow overarm stroke, her dark head submerged in the milky water; she saw him too, and altered her course, coming in some way up the shore, and disappearing into the reeds without a glance at him. He decided to walk back up the hill for his sitting. On the path through the poplars he again met Duff and Varna going down for a bathe. They stopped and talked for a moment. 'Coming to the gala?' said Varna. 'It's shorts tonight.'

'Yes. I should love to.'

'What are you doing now? Why don't you join us?'

'I have to go and sit to Rascasse, for my portrait. By the way, what do you think of him?'

He felt like a doctor discussing a bad case with matron. Duff slouched acquiescent beside her.

'Well, two years ago I thought he was a very good painter. Now I'm not so sure. He certainly hasn't improved. I'm afraid he's rather a waster. This place isn't very good for you unless you've some work to do. It gets you down.'

She was at him again. The matron who won't let the doctor slip up. 'I know,' he answered. 'Too many of your galas I expect.' He went on by the main street. The taxi had gone. Rascasse was mixing his colours when he arrived.

'Well, well, you dog, so that's the way the land lay. Take care you don't start a Corsican vendetta.'

'Oh, shut up.'

'Sorry, old pal – gee, I laughed when you went off in that taxi. My! Toni was furious. She never spoke afterwards.'

'What did you do?'

'Oh, we went up to John Foster's place. There was just him and Sonia and the colonial.'

'Who's the colonial?'

'Oh, he's a little guy that's been a lot in the colonies. He's about fifty and dances about all the time to show how young he feels. He's an old friend of Sonia's. Well, old boy, so you're not sore with Rascasse any more!' He settled down to the painting. The evening before and the night in the open had not been without their effect on Naylor's features. Rascasse kept peering at his bloodshot eyes and exhausted mouth while he made the necessary corrections. 'Gee – I thought your eyes were bigger – little mistakes like that can ruin a portrait. Once you get one proportion wrong all the other things follow.' Naylor did not protest, but sat looking out of the window, listless. Was Varna right? Was he really changing? He was freer; his mind had broadened since he came to Trou, he was less of an English molly, less of a Wykehamist. Was there anything else? He knew nothing of Mediterranean madness, of the altered tissues which are associated with the *zone nerveuse*, the arid foreshore of that iodine-charged littoral. There is a form of local madness to be caught in every region. In the country a certain grossness, an infectious stupidity; in London a social insanity which takes the form, when anybody's name is mentioned, of automatically remarking when we last saw them. In the south there is perhaps some glandular alteration. Everybody becomes rather balmy, and yet the balminess, which usually appears not only as great moral toleration but as an almost drunken ethical laxity (everybody is 'beautiful', 'wonderful characters', 'so brave', 'she couldn't be nicer if she tried') gives way to unexpected acts of violence, brawls, rapes, killings, and other escapades, till suddenly all is redissolved into gossip and easy tears. This rhythm is at the root of the monotony to be found in all mediterranean chronicles, which relate nothing but one side or both of protracted quarrels and love-affairs, there being but little else to describe. The behaviour, which is typical, we are told, of actors at home, becomes, out there, for a time the universal code. What rendered his Rock Pool so attractive to Naylor, however, was the note of archaism, the obsolete forms to be found within it. Sicily, Capri, Majorca, Brioni, Corfu, all the island colonies of eccentric Anglo-Saxons, were, since the slump, one with Homburg and Spa: in Capri the untrimmed ilexes spread over Marsac's marble palace; the outraged Majorcans had gaoled or exiled such picturesque characters as had descended on Palma and Pollensa; the Sicilian youth walked unmolested in Taormina and Cefalu. Here alone a spark of life survived; a life moreover that belonged to the period when people could still keep out of politics, when a change of government did not recall them to their citizenship by a change of income. The people who were left in Trou did not have any income: by an economic law the men had been the first to go and, as in Capri, the women, whose alimony came more regularly than their brothers' allowances, had taken possession. But, unlike Capri, the site was not sufficiently beautiful for them to be driven out by paschal hordes of Germans or summering duchesses. They were individualists, but they hadn't got the money to parade their individuality, and

consequently to decorate it with the posturing common to
those cocktail parties in expensive villas, where revel the
self-exiled grand-children of the self-made. On the hill at
Trou they rather resembled beautiful cave-dwellers sup-
porting in hieratic and traditional raggedness a dying religion while underneath them went on nothing but brib-
ery, politics, and the making of money.

He was beginning to hear more from Rascasse and the
others about those hardy hillmen who had left before the
women's invasion. There was Antheil the musician, a
captivating young man who was the village's only claim to
a celebrity and who had remained, in spite of money and
his success as a composer, oddly faithful to it. There was
Bob Brown, a retired business man, who had invented a
reading machine and a special prose tickertape. There was
a character called Link of whom the French waiter in the
café told endless stories. He had induced his friends to
spend an evening there and told the manager he would
bring them back the next night if he got free drinks. Then
he had taken them the night after to another café. 'The
manager of The Select gives me free drinks,' he said. 'I'll
make all my friends go to you in return for free drinks and
dinner.' He had see-sawed up and down between the two
till all his meals and drinks were provided, for persuading
his friends to return every night to the original one. He had
left for America very suddenly owing about twenty
thousand francs, in an old mackintosh with a bottle of *fine*
sticking out of one pocket and a roll of diabetic's bread
from the other. The waiter seemed especially pleased
about the money. '*Vingt mille francs! Ah, c'était un type,
vous savez.*'

Now that Naylor was obviously not anxious to marry
Toni, Rascasse was less guarded in his references to her.
He preferred to talk of Sonia. 'She's a wonderful girl. She
comes and kisses me good-morning every day. Today I

said: "But I can't let you kiss me, Sonia, till I've cleaned my teeth", but she said: "Oh, never mind about your teeth, Rascasse," and kissed me just the same. I'm just a little bit in love with her.'

'Is she in love with you?'

'No, but she's sorry for me, because she's a virgin and so she tries to make it up to me.'

'Well, that's something.'

'Yes, but she's sorry for the colonial too, because he takes her everywhere in his car.'

'He finds her a virgin as well?'

'Yes, but she doesn't know what to do about him – and then Toni doesn't want to go to Spain any more.'

'What does Toni want?'

'Well, that little kid jus' doesn't . . .'

At that moment she came in. One of Naylor's most redeeming and un-English traits was that he had a genuine love of visual beauty. When he saw that radiant Etruscan figure he realized that her good looks were their own justification, and he could not find it possible to be angry with her. The balminess took hold of him, like snow on wool. 'Sit down, my sweet little Toni, and tell me how you're feeling.'

To his surprise she burst into tears. 'Oh, I'm so nervous – what shall I do? – it makes me so nervous being near him.'

'Tell me about it.'

Rascasse, tactful, went on whistling and painting.

'It's John – John Foster. He wants his wife to divorce him. He wants to marry me, a *mariage blanc*, you understand, and go and live in Borneo. His wife won't come back till he has decided.'

'But she's in Italy.'

'No, she's not, she's here in the mountains at . . .' she checked herself.

'Well, what do you want to do?'

60

'I don't know.'

'And why a *mariage blanc*?'

'Oh, because he knows I would never sleep with him.'

'Then what's the trouble?'

'Oh, it makes me so nervous. I can't bear to have a man so near – always puffing and panting. I can't bear it. I can't bear it.'

'Well, then, I certainly shouldn't marry him. If you want my advice,' he went on, 'no man in his senses would enter into a *mariage blanc* with a woman unless he had no intention of keeping it. If he's in love with you, he'll expect to sleep with you – that's the end of it.'

'Foster is a man of honour,' interrupted Rascasse. 'He is an ancient Scottish gentleman.'

'I don't believe he's ever been to Scotland.'

'Of course he has,' said Toni, 'He lives in Skye. I was there last summer, staying with him.'

Naylor felt he was getting unpopular.

'You don't understand,' she went on, 'I cannot bear a man to be near me, it makes me ill – but I am so sorry for him.'

'Haven't you got some woman friend you can ask – what about Sonia?'

'Oh, she wants me to go with him, of course.'

'Well, someone older?'

'Ah – but I couldn't ask *Her* – if only I could ask: "Shall I go or shall I stay? If I stay shall I ever be able to speak to you? If I go it will be because you bid me!" If only I could speak to her – but when I go up there I am too frightened. I never can get beyond the fountain.'

'Who do you mean – do you mean the fountain of Saint-Pierre?'

'Yes, yes, of course – don't you know – I mean Princess Rustchuk – what do you think? – why should I live in Saint-Pierre last year – but I dare not, I dare not.'

He felt grateful. At last he was in on something, had been given some news before the others. He must help her.

'Doesn't Princess Rustchuk cook dinners in her café.'

'Yes, she does.'

'Well, you go up to Saint-Pierre and ask her to get dinner for four tonight. Something quite simple; then wait for us there. She'll have to talk to you about that. Then you can ask her.'

'Oh, thank you.' She walked up and kissed him on the cheek.

'I hope you'll join me for dinner, Rascasse.'

'Sure.'

Toni had gone.

'Well, fancy that, Rascasse!'

'Yes. But it was mean of you to talk like that about Foster – of course he tried to get Toni to go with him and his wife back to Borneo but his wife wasn't having any, so she took the child and went up to . . . But I promised not to say where.'

'But you didn't know about Princess Rustchuk?'

'Didn't know about Princess Rustchuk! Why, we teased that little kid so much about Princess Rustchuk that she went off to Corsica. And you took her a ticket for the dancers! Have you noticed the light that comes into her eye when she's talking to a woman – any woman – it's like a Catholic trying to make a convert; why, she even got Lola to leave the Corsican for two nights. It's the only thing she cares about.'

'Where does she get money from?'

'She hasn't any money.'

'But where does she get it when she has?'

'Why, from Foster of course, he's been giving it her for two years – anything else you want to know?'

'Yes, where do you wash?'

'Wash? Oh, under the pump. Just look over to the right a little more, please.'

That seemed to have answered most of his questions. He considered them while the sitting was progressing. It explained why she wouldn't go on to the dancers after having got him up to Saint-Pierre for dinner. What did the princess look like? She was dark and beefy, he called to mind, but not as embarrassing-looking as the dancer whom she resembled. Handsome, tougher, not so morbid, not so yellow. She seemed a curious lodestar for Toni to guide her existence by. What did Foster think of her?

'By the way, what is Mrs Foster like?' he asked.

'Oh, well, she's an American, rather pretty, rather chic, but very uneasy. She's always trying to show off to Foster that she can do without him. Her face isn't as good as it was but she's got a beautiful figure. She's one of those cold lecherous little flirts with too much make-up. She was around the coast quite a bit before she married him. She's of a very good old Baltimore family, but not as old as his, of course; she's always trying a little too hard to make people like her.'

'What's she really doing now? What does she think of Foster and Toni?'

'Well, she quite likes Toni, because Toni tried to make her leave Foster at first – you know how little Toni can't bear to see a woman with a man.'

'I thought it was a man with a woman.'

'O hell! Anyhow when Foster fell so hard for Toni she thought he'd get a lesson, but when she found that he didn't mind her being queer, that he didn't ask for anything at all, she was much more upset, and then in Skye it turned out that she didn't really like primitive people and Toni did and they began to leave her at home and then she minded quite a lot; then Toni turned up here.'

'When was that?'

'About a week before I met you and we saw her at the Bastion.'

63

'What did she come here for?'

'Why, she came to meet Sonia to go to Spain with her. Besides, she was broke.'

'You mean she came to get Foster to give her some money to go to Spain with Sonia?'

'Yes. I told you she was broke.'

'Well, why doesn't she go?'

'Because she really came to be near Princess Rustchuk.'

'Why did Mrs Foster leave him then?'

'Because he suggested they should take Toni to Borneo – he's crazy about her.'

'Why Borneo?'

'What a guy you are for asking questions. The natives invited him. Don't you know about Foster and the Dyaks! He got them out of some sort of a jam with the government and they asked him to be their resident – then Mrs Foster said he must choose between her and Toni and she went up to the mountains.'

'So he chose Toni and now she won't have him?'

'Say, what are you? A private detective?'

Naylor nodded and lowered his eyelids – a trick he had. 'Yes,' he articulated preciously, 'yes.'

They couldn't find Lola to ask her to make a fourth, and Naylor refused to let Rascasse bring Sonia. 'Not till I'm introduced.' For once they caught a bus and reached Saint-Pierre while the walled village was still amiable in the westering sun. They waited in the café outside the walls for a little and had several *fines-à-l'eau*, Naylor had a sudden inspiration, he saw himself as an irresistible seducer since the night before, a mixture of Rochester, Richelieu, and Gramont. The reflections on Foster's superior birth continually stung him and here was a way to be revenged. He would find out which mountain resort his wife was staying in, and then, when he officially departed the next day for England, he would sneak up there.

Obviously she would be bored stiff. It would be easy to get to know her, some champagne would do the rest, and she would return a few days later to taunt Foster with the unknown lover. She would describe him – he would give a false name, of course – and finally the horrible truth would dawn on her husband – cuckolded by a WYKEHAMIST! He might even run away with her and leave Foster stuck with Toni. He smiled and nodded over his brandy, flicking his thumbs in his Hamlet way. 'Yes. Yes. Yes.'

'Yes, what?'

'Oh nothing, Rascasse, just that I'm going away to-morrow. My investigation is closed.'

'And whom do you suspect, Mr Van Dine?'

'I suspect everybody.'

'And what then?'

'I hope very shortly to make an arrest.'

'Well, that's too bad. We'll never have that walk to La Gaude.'

Naylor looked up at the brown village high in the pine woods, and then across at Vence where the lights began to flicker in the sanatoriums. There Lawrence died.

'Mrs Foster's at Vence, isn't she?'

'No.'

'Am I hot or cold?'

'Cold.'

'She's at Magnanosc.'

'She's where?'

He gave it up. They strolled on towards the princess'. Night was falling like a camera shutter, already the walls of Saint-Pierre were growing cold and forbidding. Lacking the harlotry of Trou the village seemed to frown with mediaeval austerity on the exotic creatures within it. The air was purer, the conditions rougher, the female marriages more permanent up here. When they reached the 'Sarment de Vigne' Toni was waiting for them. He looked more closely at the café. The walls were coloured off-white, and hung with paintings, or rather abstract ornaments in which configurations of rusty wire, bright pieces of tin and cotton wool and cork predominated. Naylor searched in vain for a signature or a price ticket which might help him to tell if they were the real thing. The princess came forth like an indignant Artemis about to transform Actaeon.

'*Le dîner sera prêt dans quarante-cinq minutes.*'

'*Mais c'est commandé – qu'est-ce que vous avez?*'

'*Il y aura un potage paysanne, des œufs, des côtes de mouton, de la salade et du fromage. Le prix sera cinquante francs par personne.*'

'*Cinquante francs! C'est ridicule. C'est plus que le Ritz.*'

The princess stiffened. '*Vous oubliez, monsieur, que je suis un cordon bleu, et puis, je ne fais pas des repas pour tout le monde. Ça ne me donne aucun plaisir de faire de la cuisine, vous comprenez.*'

'*Mais cinquante francs! et puis il ne faut pas être cordon bleu pour faire des œufs et une salade.*'

'*Parfaitement, monsieur, à votre place je dirais la même chose. C'était seulement parce que la petite me l'a demandé que j'ai consenti à faire le repas. Evidemment il y avait un malentendu: elle devait vous renseigner d'avance sur les prix. C'est facile à décommander, j'espère que vous trouverez mieux ailleurs.*'

'*Mais j'ai commanDÉ . . .*'

'*Ne discutez pas, monsieur, je vous en prie.*'

She turned away and began muttering to her blonde partner who emerged from the door as they left it, carrying back to the butcher's four bleeding chops. They went across to the hotel where they had dined on the night of the dancers. Rascasse talked little. He seemed to think Naylor had behaved very badly indeed. Toni was silent. His treat for her hadn't amounted to much, he reflected, and then the private detective in him began to wonder what her rake-off would have been. Or was he making a mistake in dealing with these people, in assuming that because they had no money and were delighted to take his, that they were consequently mercenary and up to the petty chisellings of a French hotelkeeper? Perhaps they were simply ignorant of the tabus attaching to gold.

'*On voyait que c'était une vraie princesse*,' Rascasse summed up, and Toni giggled happily.

'I've certainly never heard a real cook say she disliked cooking as an excuse for overcharging,' said Naylor, and Rascasse remarked that it was just a question of knowing how to get on with these people, as it was with ordinary ones.

'How often do you entertain, Rascasse?'

'Really, Naylor, I am sorry you should ask that question', he began. Toni stopped suddenly and stamped on the pavement. 'My ancestors entertained,' she exclaimed, 'oh, exquisitely, exquisitely – my great-grandfather asked all the nobles of Hungary, Courland and Moravia to visit him and built a special palace for them beside his own and a large house for the servants. They stayed for three weeks and there was hunting all day and feasting every night to his private orchestra and when they went away he had to sell sixty thousand hectares and the lordship of Ada Kaleh to pay for it.'

'Then where did he live?'

'Oh, he lived in Chicago.'

Both Rascasse and Naylor were grateful to her. They passed the Roseraie; in an arbour under the lanterns in the orange trees Sonia was dining with her colonial friend. Her birchwood hair shone above her golden face. She still wore white duck trousers and a white shirt. The colonial's grizzled head was wagging. Beside them, surrounded by admiring waiters, an expensive kind of sweet was exploding in flames.

'Poor little Sonia!' said Rascasse, 'she has to put up with a lot.'

At dinner Rascasse addressed the air. 'Nobody can touch my pride, you understand; I am a painter and a good painter. Nobody has to tell me. I know it. When I have money I spend it. Nobody gives better parties than I do, but when I have none, I don't grumble. I go without. I have gone for days with nothing to eat and I've been through winters in Paris without an overcoat. When I'm broke I *mean* I'm broke – not waiting a few days for a cheque and borrowing from my hotel, but penniless, starving, with nothing, you understand, and I put up with insults, with every sort of degradation. I get myself despised by people who are nothing, by these vile little second-rate fairies here, simply because their belly is fuller or because they are better dressed, but my pride is inviolate. Nobody can touch my pride.' He glared at Naylor.

'No, I'm sure they can't.'

'All right then, now we're pals. Shake!'

After the reconciliation, he went across the road to talk to Sonia, ostensibly to see if the colonial would take them all back to Trou in his car. Naylor was alone, for the first time since he had known her, with Toni.

'Well, what did the princess say?'

'Oh, you see, I didn't dare ask her.'

'I don't see, if Foster gets on your nerves so, why you want to go to Borneo at all.'

'Because of the job.'

'?'

'Don't you understand? I must have a job. I want to work, to earn my living, anything, and he promises I can learn farming, in Borneo.'

'What sort of farming?'

'Any kind – tropical farming, I suppose.'

'But why should you go and fall for that job stuff; you're perfectly all right without one.'

'No, till last year I was all right. I never thought about money, but now it's not the same and I mayn't do journalism any more, because I'm not a German subject.'

'Can't Mrs Foster get you a job in America?'

'I suppose so – but if I go with them to Borneo, the Dyaks will pay my fare.'

'Oh, I see – and where is Mrs Foster?'

'She's up in the mountains – I can't say where.'

'Toni – aren't you rather ungrateful?'

'Why?'

'You've never thanked me for that two hundred francs.'

'What two hundred francs?'

'I gave Rascasse two hundred francs to give you for sitting to him.'

'He never said anything about it.'

'Really! By the way, Toni, where do you wash?'

'Why, at Foster's'.

'Do many people wash there?'

'Only Sonia and me and Rascasse sometimes.'

'He said he washed under the pump.'

'The pump is rather dry. I thought you meant where do we use the toilette.'

'How long have you been in love with Princess Rustchuk?'

'Two years. Oh, I can't bear it any longer – she never even speaks to me – her friend forbids her. It is ruining my life. If it wasn't for her I might have a job and be happy.'

'If only you were normal, you could get married and you wouldn't have to think about jobs and princesses.'

'Well, what is that to do with it?'

'I don't believe you are really queer. I think you just don't know what you want.'

'Oh, shut up, you silly, ridiculous – I have been like that since I was five, you understand, everybody says that to me sooner or later. I've *never* had anything to do with a man. Why, even in Skye they asked me to leave because I was interfering with the wives of the fishermen!'

'I'm sorry, I was only being helpful. . . .'

'It's quite all right.'

'Can't you go off with Sonia?'

'We haven't enough money. It is so difficult.'

'But you've done trips with her before?'

'No, never.'

'How long have you known her?'

'Only three or four days. Why, you saw us at the Bastion the day she got here.'

'You mean to say she came to stay with you without ever having met you?'

'Yes, of course.'

'Tell me about it.'

'Well – oo – you see – aah – my brother, the one who is a dancer, had a friend in Munich. And he gave his friend my photograph. And the friend is a very good-looking, very athletic man. And he always pretended to be very much in love with me and showed my photograph to the girls in Munich who were in love with him at the university, to excuse himself, and he showed Sonia my photograph, and then she thought she would like me for a friend, so she wrote and said we were the same age and she was sure we would be very good friends and asked where I was and sent the letter to my brother, and so I said to tell her I was in Skye. And so she walked to Skye, but when she got there she found I had just left. She stayed with the Fosters a little and then walked to London, and there I had just left too, so she went back to Germany, and wrote again and then I said I was in Trou and she suggested we should go to Spain so she walked here. That is all.'

'Where did she find you?'

'I was sitting on the terrace at the top of the hill and she came up.'

'You knew it was her?'

'Well, she had a rucksack on her back.'

'What did she say?'

'She came over and kissed me and said: *"Also du bist Toni?"* '

'And then?'

'Then I said she must be tired and I took her to my room, and I said I was afraid it was very dirty, but she looked around the room, and said: "What a pretty ceiling", then we had dinner with Foster and she got tight.'

Rascasse came back. 'The colonial is very sorry. He doesn't think he has room in his car for more than four – so one of us must go by bus.'

'Let's all go by bus.'

'He says there's always room for Toni.'

'I think perhaps it would hurt his feelings if I didn't go,' said Toni. 'Besides, Sonia is very anxious not to be alone with him in the car.'

'O.K.,' said Rascasse, 'maybe I ought to go too?'

He saw Naylor glaring at him. He wouldn't be able to get away with it. 'Yes, maybe I ought – sure, I know I ought, but I'd a damn sight rather stay with you, Naylor, even if we have to walk down.'

'Then we will walk down.'

Toni departed to the car. They set off down the road.

'Oh by the way, Rascasse, did you remember to give Toni that two hundred francs?'

'No, why should I give her two hundred francs, if she won't sit for me! Besides, she owes me two hundred francs, so we're all square.'

'You mean you've spent it?'

'No, I was keeping it for you. I thought you'd want to put it towards your picture.'

'How much is the picture?'

'Well, I'll make it, for you, a thousand francs – then you've paid me four hundred francs of it.'

'Supposing I don't like it?'

'Oh, you'll like it. Everybody likes Rascasse's portraits.'

'Very well then.'

They walked on in silence.

'That is my fatal error,' went on Rascasse, 'the characteristic which is so profoundly prejudicial to my interests, that stands between me and success.'

'What is?'

'I do not like to mention money. I hate to bargain. I hate to name a price. Why, if I was to say what my pictures are worth, I would say five thousand, ten thousand. But there is something inherently repugnant in me which will not do it. An artist today should be a business man. I am not one.'

'How much further is it?'

'About seven kilometres.'

'Don't you think it's going to rain?'

'Maybe.'

'It wouldn't do to get wet.'

'Let's take the bus then.'

Luckily one was passing. As they got to the Bastion it really did rain. The gala was in full swing and the deluge outside improved it. People came running in in pairs with shining cheeks and wet hair, as if they were going aboard the ark. There was a smell of wet earth, the water plopped on the heavy fig leaves; the lavatories of Trou, of which the Bastion's was one of the proudest, flushed and snorted. Everybody looked clean and tropical in their shorts. Duff and Varna went about smiling with huge trays of glasses. It was the period when people were still arriving, when they were filling themselves with drink and still waiting in the wings for the roles their intoxicated selves were to play. Naylor was once more reminded of the charming primitiveness of most of them. They all looked so rosy, innocent and happy, that they might have been backwoods trappers and lumbermen come in to some frontier town for a Saturday night. They looked as if they would pay for their drinks from silver belts or little bags of gold dust. As before, there were hardly any men. Eddie-from-the-top, tall, ugly and disagreeable, the Corsican, the unfrocked priest, small and pasty, and John Foster, with Sonia's colonial; the stag-line was complete. The women had mostly arrived in couples from outlying cottages, and there was the usual contingent from Trou. Lola greeted him affectionately. The woman in the apache clothes growled: 'Aren't you going to say good-evening to me?' and shifted her pipe across her mouth. Toni brought Sonia up and introduced him. 'I have heard so much about you,' she said. 'Tell me, why do you come here if you are such a snob?'

'Who said I was a snob?'

'Why, everybody. John Foster, Ruby, Rascasse, Varna. I'm sure it must be very amusing.' She brushed a raindrop from her cheek, and stood looking at him with her hands in the pockets of her white trousers.

He felt old and miserable, going through life trying to peddle a personality of which people would not even accept a free sample. He remembered the parties he had frequented in London. Fiddling about with the bookshelves or the plates of biscuits while everybody turned their back or seemed to recognize him only at the last possible moment. There are times when the fear of life is greater than the fear of death, when the remaining years, forty or fifty of them, stretch out ahead like the steps of an infinitely tiring staircase. Sonia took one look at his long empty face. She felt for the first time the proximity of some ancient enemy of youth and spirit, and moved quietly away.

There was a stir in the porch; he raised his eyes. Jimmy came in, heavily made up and more platinoid than ever, and with him the beautiful girl he had seen in the café at Juan. She wore the same white canvas shorts, laughing vapidly, and seemed perfectly content with her escort. Round them circled the unfrocked priest, the girl with the piqûres on her arm, who was wearing a man's thick woollen shirt, and her plump redheaded friend. Their entrance caused a kind of restlessness at the bar. Varna and Duff retired into a corner and began whispering. When Varna brought him his drink he asked for information.

'Oh, those two,' she said. 'We'd like to turn them out, only I don't for a moment suppose they'd go. That's Geraldine, the fat red-head – do you know what she did? She came into the kitchen the last time she was here while I was scrambling some eggs. I didn't hear her and she walked right up behind me and bit me in the neck. It got infected too.' He noticed the knots of a bandage showing under her high-necked sweater and felt more cheerful.

'Who is the other?'

'That's Dicky. She's had D.T.'s three times. They live in the woods near Antibes. She's terrible too, but Geraldine's really wicked. She's married but separated from her husband. She makes money by teaching people to dope. She gets paid by the traffickers.'

He asked Varna to have a drink with him. She talked on about Geraldine, the mischief she made, her trick of leading people on till she could make them in some way ridiculous, how she could be charming when she wanted. Varna was the only person in Trou who talked to him naturally, as an equal. Behind her words he caught a glimpse of real character, some one with courage and self-respect, who worked hard under enormous difficulties, was kind, trustful and energetic. It didn't make him like her any better. He felt mean and envious. She had no business to be a nice person. Nobody wants to be reminded of such standards, he thought; no wonder she gets a bite in the neck.

There are so few wicked people in the world; the springs of vanity, fear, envy, cupidity and deceit, while sources of the general nastiness of human beings, do not make for moral evil on a grand scale. Consequently a really dangerous person, a genuine ill-doer and not merely an ill-wisher to the human race, is an object of fascination. As with a bad-tempered animal or a difficult child, everyone feels they can do something with them. (Oh, he won't hurt ME) and, since there are about forty-nine masochists to one sadist, they never want for victims. Naylor was soon able to edge his way along the bar to Geraldine and give her a light for her cigarette. She had a rakish musical voice, a babyish prettiness, the wide sensual mouth of a Rowlandson whore, and was not yet too fat to be attractive. She looked closely at him when she smiled, like a large cat that had just eaten, he thought, and at once made him feel that they were both enjoying a private joke about the whole evening.

'Did you ever see such an extraordinary collection?' she said. 'I didn't know there were such people − not your friend − the little one in Tirolese costume. She's charming, of course; but it's all rather queer after Cap d'Antibes. By the way, who is she?'

'Would you like to meet her?'

'Yes, you must both come out and dine with me one day and I'll try to get some amusing people.'

It was the first time he had been invited to anything and he was delighted. He brought Toni over and introduced her. It appeared that Geraldine knew Courland intimately. He moved away as she was exclaiming: 'Why, we must be some sort of cousins, then!' and collided with Jimmy. 'There you are, you little rat, why didn't you come to tea with me yesterday?'

'I did, only you never turned up.'

'Well, you can't expect everything, don't be grasping! Tahiti, let me present to you one of my oldest and dearest friends, a Mr . . ., anyhow, he's an English boy and he has spent the most gangrenous youth!' Naylor asked her to dance and pushed her around with set face. He didn't like to talk while he was dancing; for him it was like driving through traffic, but she chatted a little. She was a dancer; her grandmother had been queen of Tahiti, her father was an Australian boot manufacturer, she had been 'fabulously wealthy'. She was staying at Juan-les-Pins for a holiday. Her husband hoped to join her. She asked him to come round and see her at her hotel the next day, about lunch-time. He could hardly believe that anyone so attractive could bother to be nice to him and revived enormously. He went to get her a drink. Geraldine bumped heavily into him, she was very excited. 'Beg your pot-pot,' she ex-claimed. 'Oh, it's you – have you seen my little Hungarian bitch anywhere?'

Toni was going round the tables, giggling and pointing at Geraldine while she shrugged her shoulders with an 'as Allah wills' effect.

'She's not Hungarian,' said Naylor.

'I don't care what she is. Oh, there you are.'

Toni arrived smirking, and Geraldine put a fat freckled arm round her. At the same moment it was snatched away and she was confronted by her friend Dicky; the coarse wool shirt was open at the neck, her face was grey with alcohol, she had once been handsome, with the good looks of a dilapidated Roman emperor. Now her eyes were blood-shot, her mouth hung open.

'Darling, you do love me, don't you?' she said, and drove

her scarred fist into Gerladine's face. There was an uproar.
Geraldine sat on the floor weeping; Dicky remained
wiping her mouth on her sleeve; Toni scuttled off to John
Foster, who stood up to protect her. Tahiti was dancing a
rumba by herself. She ended with the splits, laughing inanely, and upset a tableful of glasses as she came down.
Jimmy towered over her.

'You did it, Naylor, you tripped her up.'

'I didn't.'

'Now remember, Mr Manners, don't contradict.'

'I had nothing whatever to do with it. She fell down
because she couldn't stand up.'

'In fact I'm a liar?'

'No, not for a moment.'

'You little English queen, you horrify me; the salacity of
the boy!'

'Let me go.'

'Say manners maketh queens.'

'No.'

'Say it.'

'Ouch, for God's sake, let go.'

'Say it.'

'Very well, if you must be so childish, manners maketh
queens.'

'Thank you – manners, of course, in the broadest sense.'

Naylor sped away up the street. The man was a degener-
ate bully. He decided to go up to the terrace. The rain had
stopped, the gutters sang with descending water as he
climbed in the dark; clouds moved behind the Grimaldi
towers, obscuring the moon. The terrace was deserted but
he saw a light in Eddie's bar. There was no one there but
Eddie and Lola. Eddie served him unwillingly. He tried to
join in the conversation.

'Excuse me,' said the barman, 'but may I ask you a
personal question?'

'Certainly.'

'Just who the hell are you?'

'I am a friend of Lola's.'

'And how do you happen to combine a syphilitic nose in a Semitic face?'

'Look here – I say!'

'You understand, as a customer, I am delighted to serve you. I'm just asking you as a friend.'

'Damn you.'

'There, I'm afraid I've hurt your feelings. But remember: ladies present!'

Lola made a sympathetic grimace at him. *'Ah, vous savez, il est entièrement saoul.'*

Eddie said: 'That's it. Take you for a drive – fresh air, soon feel better.' He walked out holding Lola's arm.

Naylor followed. The car was outside on the square. He saw Lola pushed into it. The Norwegian American turned to him. 'Get in.'

'I say, can you drive all right?'

'Get in.'

'Oui – venez – j'ai tellement peur de rester seule avec lui.'

It did not occur to him that if she felt like that she needn't go at all. He would stay with them, perhaps Eddie would pass out and then he could go home with her again. Eddie handed him a bottle of whisky and he took a long drink. They rushed up the mountain road, Eddie driving and Naylor hugging Lola in the back. At an open space Eddie turned and stopped. They had some more whisky. When they tried to re-start the car nothing happened. 'Can't start,' mumbled the American, 'Battery.' He slumped forward in his seat. 'Somebody got to wind.'

Naylor got out and wound the handle. The motor caught, the car shot forward, knocking him over, and slid down the road. He lay where he fell. It seemed as good a place to sleep as any. When he woke it was the middle of the morning. It had been his second night in the open. His face was cut; his intolerable headache he owed to the usual cause. He walked slowly down into Trou. Eddie's bar was closed. The Rock Pool was sleeping; a few shrimpy children played in the street, and as he got to Rascasse's door a wan and vaguely familiar figure passed him. It was a pale strawy little girl, carrying a Pernod bottle. Of course, he remembered, Ruby's daughter gone to fetch her breakfast.

VI

RASCASSE was already painting. 'Well, well, the last sitting. Let's get down to it. This is going to be a great picture. Just let me put in those lines round the mouth. My! You can see what Trou has done to you, I've never seen anyone so altered. The ravages! It reminds me of the *Picture of Dorian Gray*, only it's the other way round; my portrait can't keep pace with all the changes. That's a profound book – a work of profound truth and quasi-similitude. "To cure the soul by means of the senses, and the senses by means of the soul." Can you beat it! The formula of the artist's life in a nutshell. Yes. Oscar Wilde – a fairy but a wonderful guy. So you're really going to leave us this evening? Had enough after last night! Gee, you were a fool to go and make an enemy of Jimmy. He's a dangerous chap, and it couldn't have hurt you to have had tea with him. Well, that was the last party of the season. There won't be any more now. Some party! Those two women from Antibes passed out and had to be put in Duff's bedroom. And then Tahiti! She said she'd broken her knee doing the *grand écart*, and Duff and Varna had to carry her down to the village. Imagine carrying her half a kilometre! They had to get a doctor and she screamed so when he touched her he couldn't find out if anything was the matter. Then Sonia had a row with the colonial. She told me about it when she came to say good-morning to me. By the way, John Foster has it in for you. He says that you public school and varsity men ought to stand by each other and that instead you spend all your time with Americans like Jimmy and Norwegians like Eddie-from-the-top. Toni's not going to marry him or even to go to Borneo. She feels it her duty to stay and help Geraldine. Well, I guess that's finished now.'

They both stood back to look at the picture. Against an oyster background the haggard face was only too effective. Handsome but ravaged with weakness and gloom, it might have been of some cashiered aviator, the features, young, pale, and almost noble, were forgotten, when you looked at the eyes, two wells of hopelessness, and the fallen jaw.

'Pretty swell, eh! I think I've earned my thousand francs.'

'I admire it immensely. I'll call round for it this evening before my train goes, and give you the rest of the money.'

'Splendid, the varnish will be dry then and you can pack it easier. I'll be down at the hotel café with it at six o'clock.'

'God, I feel bad.'

'Take a swim – that'll improve you.'

He caught a crowded bus back to Juan, in which he had to stand all the way, and his cuts and two days' growth caused him to be unpleasantly stared at. He was one of those inverted Samsons who lose all their strength till they have been shorn of their beard, and could only hang his head. After a shave he was well enough to face the hotel. They were quite pleased to see him but his correspondence was not reassuring. His bank made it clear that he had only twenty pounds to his credit till the end of November and there was one of those tiresome pinpricking letters by which old friends ease the bonds of expiring friendship. It was from John Spedding. 'What has happened to you? Aren't you ever coming back! I can't believe that research into the life (if you can call life that long abstention from experience) of the Banker Bard has detained you so long in those flowery fields. Are you by any chance becoming the Don Juan of the Pines? I dined with George Bowler at the Escargot the other day. We both wondered what had happened to you and agreed how lucky you were to be able to afford the flesh-pots of Monte Carlo (though they must be a little tawdry by the end of September) when we were both sweating away in the metropolis. Bowler is very much the coming man, and little Kerr has been made Bensonian lecturer. We all went down to the old school the other day and found College very much the same. Nobody enquired after you. What have you done to upset Maurice? I was down at Oxford last week-end and he was in a great state about something – "one of my more delible errors", he called you, but I seem always to be fighting your battles. Old Squeers, at All Souls, asked after you and said he was beginning to doubt whether such a person as Rogers ever existed. No other news. David's Wordsworth is out; he makes great play of Fox's "Mr Wordsworth, I am not of your faction", which apparently was said at Rogers's and led to R. boosting Crabbe instead – but you probably know more about this than he does. There have been no new names for my collection – Pine-coffin, Trampleasure, Jolly d'Aeth are getting so hackneyed. I haven't seen "the Fretful Porpentine" for ages. He seems to have disappeared completely. I have been to a few small routs – nobody's you would know, but am too busy with my briefs to go out very much. Well, good-bye and write to me soon. I do hope you haven't got into what our dear tutor used to call "a fast set" and that you are profitably enjoying your –? holiday. (You remember how he used

to say, "Naylor, it's no good you getting the idea that you
can two-step through life".)

> Yours ever,
> JOHN.

'*P.S.* – Bowler says Davenports are going to pass their
dividend. I believe you have some, but I'm afraid this will
reach you too late.'

Whew! He remembered their friendship at school. They
had sat next each other and held hands over a copy of Latin
verses.

> Little brown brother, little brown brother,
>> Are you awake in the dark?
> Here we lie cosily close to each other,
>> Hark to the song of the lark!
>
>> *(Ecce carmen alaudae)*

It had given them a sentimental erotic thrill, though from
the rest of the poem it had turned out to be a potato talking.
It was a long journey from the security of the class-room to
the appalling liberty of Trou, from the brown brothers to
Tahiti. Spedding had simply exchanged the Gothic quads,
dining-halls, gowns, subfusc pleasures and gregarious intolerance of Winchester and Oxford for those of the law-
courts. He would never leave the quadrangle. Naylor remembered a phrase of Lytton Strachey's – 'the pedantry of
incomplete academic persons' – and felt better. He walked
down to Tahiti's hotel. She was sitting surrounded by men
but recognized him at once and made room for him beside
her. She was still in her shorts, with a large white bandage
round her brown knee. She went on talking about her
experiences: 'and then I felt a terrible searing pain and the
next thing I knew I was being carried down the hill by two
awful women and I screamed and screamed and screamed'.
Gradually the men drifted away to lunch and they were

alone. They had lunch at her hotel. She explained that all she inherited from her Tahitian grandmother were her teeth, which were very small and regular and came from chewing sharkskin. She talked mostly about the fortune she had got through when she first came to Europe. Afterwards she planned the day. 'We'll do some shopping and then we'll go into Cannes and you'll take me out to dinner. Now go and telephone and get two rooms with baths at the Miramar. I suppose you have a car?'

'No, as a matter of fact, I haven't. I find the buses are just as good.'

'Well, go hire one then – I'm not going anywhere in a bus with my knee, if you don't mind.'

When the rooms were booked and the car sent for he began to feel less optimistic. While they were waiting for it they strolled towards the beach. She walked with an exaggerated limp, with her arm round his neck for support and attracted, laughing so bravely, considerable sympathy.

'Why, what a cute pair of shoes,' she said, stopping at a little booth called Perugia. When they came out with them he had spent a thousand francs – his fare to England. It was still very hot in the street, the café tables were deserted under their yellow awnings, the travel agencies and pyjama shops frazzled in the sun. She yawned. – 'My, I feel sleepy.'

Naylor had an idea. 'Do you mind just coming up to my room while I get some more money, we'll want a good lot, won't we?'

'Why, certainly.'

Once in his room he left her sitting on the bed, explaining he was going to cash a cheque in the office. He went downstairs to the telephone, countermanded the car and the rooms and returned. She was fast asleep. He lay down beside her and slept also. When he woke up it was dark, he could just hear the music from the open-air dancings.

Tahiti yawned, smiled, and stretched herself – she put out her arm and drew him closer. 'Now I'm going to show you how a half-caste girl can love.'

When they emerged the next evening they had vowed to reform each other; neither would touch a drop of drink, and both agreed it had been a case of love at first sight. He arranged to meet her at lunch-time the day following, ate a large dinner at his hotel and went to bed. The next morning he spent in a drowsy physical reverie and the recollection of her splendid embraces. They were going to take a trip up the mountains together, to some high village like La Gaude whose pure air and twinkling lights were a constant reproach to the littoral. Exercise, simple food, regular hours and running water would do the rest. They would come down different beings and face the dreary business of her divorce.

When he reached her hotel she was surrounded by her usual males, a Packard roadster drawn up beside them.

'Why, it's you', she cried. 'Sit down, won't you?'

It was in every respect like the first occasion he had called upon her, except that she was not drinking this time, and that when the men rose to go she went with them. A waiter brought him their bill. She waved and laughed inanely as their car turned off to Cannes. This was the worst thing that had happened to him, the *coup de grace*. He could get over the love which is inspired without encouragement or consummation; he could get over the rebuffs and humiliations experienced at the hands of rivals, for it proved him a rival too, but to be degraded to acquaintanceship after a day and a night of passionate intimacy with that pantherine torso, after listening to her childish professions of love and regret, it was more than he could bear – perhaps all the other men with her had borne it. He felt that his visit to the south had been a bullfight; Trou had been the ring, Toni and Sonia and Lola had planted their darts in him, Foster and Eddie and Jimmy had been the clumsy picadors, riding him down with their heavy goads, and now Tahiti had despatched him, with the wound which to the bull seemed like other wounds, the sword buried in his neck resembling the pics in his shoulders, the banderillas in his flanks, yet causing him suddenly to stagger and choke in his vomiting blood. The lesson he had learnt, that all of us are alone, fighting for ourselves in a world that is daily growing more savage, he would necessarily have had to acquire sometime and in some place, but at home he would have learnt it gradually, slowly encrusting himself with the gentlemanly protection of English selfishness. Here life was too crude, too brutal, he had run in a couple of weeks the course in disillusion which for the ordinary eupeptic professional man is spread over a period of years. It had been too much for him. It was natural to want to go to bed with people, natural to be fond of them before and after, yet he had picked on a community where one was likely to get one's throat cut in the process, where, like a male mantis, he was devoured inchmeal. In the stricter atmosphere of school and college where the sexual appetite had been regarded as a degraded craving, and gratification in almost any form, if detected, meant expulsion, he at least had known what the rules were – sex was wicked, women criminal, boys worse, masturbation led to a severe flogging if discovered, madness if not. It was crazy, but logical. Here every kiss, every intimacy was a reflection on the giver's toughness, and had to be lived down. He went back to the hotel and was told that Monsieur Rascasse had telephoned to ask him to come and get his picture. 'He has telephoned every day to know if you were still here.'

At lunch he counted his money. Twenty pounds in the bank to last him till the end of November, and about fifteen hundred francs, of which he owed Rascasse six hundred, and his hotel a couple more. Just enough to get back to England and then he would have to begin the search for someone to stay with. 'I was wondering if you could put me up for a few days.' He had quite a hard job as a rule getting people to have dinner with him, and he knew what the answer would be. He could go away without paying Rascasse and leave him with the picture, but he felt too deeply the need to confide in someone. Toni, he knew, would be quite unsympathetic, she would put on her little secretive smile and make some remark about everybody knowing that Tahiti did not care for men. In the bus he was continually reminded of the season ending. The luxury shops were closed. In the cheaper door-ways the proprietors stood plucking at customers, the awnings were disappearing from the hotel gardens and the bamboo screens from the open-air cabarets. The coloured lights were taken down from the palms, the nine-day mistral covered the sea and land with their autumn dust sheet and brought the puritan alps close as an extinguisher.

Pomifer autumnus fruges effunderit, et mox
  bruma recurrit iners.

Once more he was climbing the hill to Rascasse's studio: an age seemed to have passed since last he was in Trou, and at every moment that he stopped to rest he was stabbed by the ache of physical separation. A few hours ago he was sleeping with her and now it was finished. He found Rascasse and the Corsican deep in politics, while a portrait of the Corsican and his wife stood on the easel. They greeted him, but went on immediately with their argument. Naylor felt jealous, he didn't like to think that other people might sit to Rascasse. Besides he loathed politics and his ideas on the subject were simple. A Czar in Russia, a Kaiser in Germany, an Emperor in Austro-Hungary and China, the income tax at pre-war figures, and a few decent letters of introduction were all he asked for. After the

Corsican's departure Naylor poured out all his troubles. Rascasse was charmingly sympathetic, listened gravely, and shaking his head at intervals. 'You poor stiff,' he gave judgement, 'did you tell Tahiti you were broke at any time?'

'Yes, I did – when we were discussing getting married.'

'That was fatal.'

'But she can't have thought I was very rich when she first met me.'

'But you know why she went to bed with you, of course?'

'She fell in love with me.'

'O Jeese, you make me sick and tired, Naylor! Tahiti is in love with Jimmy. She thought it would make him mad if she made love to you and got you away from him. Afterwards she found he didn't mind at all, and so there was no point in going on with it.'

'And Jimmy?'

'Oh, he sticks around with her because she's got a very attractive husband.'

The life of the Rock Pool, red in tooth and claw, was once more closing round him; of what other cynical, amoral tiger-hunts was he going to be the tethered goat. He felt like one of Lawrence's American ladies who fall among Indians and find themselves sooner or later trussed up for human sacrifice.

'As to being broke, I tell you what you'll do. Leave your hotel and come and get a room at the pub in the village. Living's cheap, they've got a decent bar and you can get credit. Pay me 500 francs instead of six, and send the other hundred to me when you have it. Keep the rest, a thousand francs or so, for pocket-money. Pay your hotel bill here by cheque as long as you have any money in the bank, after that put them off and finally give them a post-dated cheque for as much as possible. You can get cigarettes, drinks, put down on it, everything. If they get tiresome, send yourself a telegram: "Did you get thousand dollars safely, please cable", or something like that, and borrow enough to skip the dump on the strength of it. I'll tell them you're a regular guy and they've got to trust you. If you have to borrow, remember there're only three people with any money in this joint. Foster, the Corsican, and Eddie-from-the-top. They support most of the population. If you prefer to borrow from a woman, Ruby gets her alimony about the middle of the month, and Duff and Varna turn the till out at the beginning. Well, well, so you're broke, eh! Who ever heard of a broke detective! Remember, it's no good trying to get tick from the natives,' he went on, 'they're pretty shy by now, and if you have to skip, skip on foot and catch the slow train at three in the morning. Gee, I wish I could be there to see you!'

'Why, aren't you staying?'

'O boy, haven't you heard? Gee, it's swell. Rascasse is going to have an exhibition. Yes, sir, *une petite exposition à Paris*. And your picture's going to be the *clou*. Everyone's going to say: *"Mais qui est ce Naylor?"* You will be famous, eh!'

'I see. When are you going?'

'Tomorrow night, with poor little Lola.'

'Lola?'

'Why, what do you know? There was the biggest bust-up at the party. You know the Corsican had never invited Lola to his house in case his wife should suspect, and the night of the party his wife asked Lola to dinner. She was ecstatic about it. She's always wanted to be friends with the wife, but afterwards the wife took her aside and said she'd known all the time about her and her husband, that she regretted it, but she knew she'd never keep him if she got jealous, and that Lola was to come back and spend the night with him. Well, after the party the Corsican couldn't find her, but some one said she'd gone off in the car with

Eddie-from-the-top and he found them in bed together. Then, of course, he discovered that Lola spent every night with Eddie before he joined her in the mornings. And there was the biggest fight. Eddie was much stronger than the Corsican but he didn't have a knife, so now he's in hospital, and they've no more use for Lola. Poor little Lola. Well, she's coming to Paris with me, she's jusalil animal.'

They went down to the hotel to make arrangements. Naylor got a room for three hundred and fifty francs a month and paid in advance which made a great impression. They sat in the garden afterwards looking at old *New Yorkers* while Rascasse tried to think of a way of winning back Tahiti. The only means by which Naylor could get her back, he summed up, was by getting rich again, and this was just what he couldn't manage. He volunteered, however, to try to see her for him. Another couple made their way in. It was Mr and Mrs Foster. She was much as Rascasse had described her. She immediately got on very well with Naylor, appreciating exactly the same brand of cerebral sexual titivation. She was trying to show off in front of her husband by little dare-devilries, looking up at him like a whipped dog with its tongue out, while he glowered or pretended not to hear her. It was a marriage like many another.

'Oh, I've had the dullest time,' she explained. 'I hadn't been feeling very well in the heat and John made me go up to a terrible little place in the hills called La Gaude, where the wine comes from. There was only one wretched café in the place and I don't know what I would have done if it hadn't been for the sweetest French officer who was up there convalescing from a fever. My husband tells me you were at Winchester. It's always so funny, I think, though, of course, I know very little about England, that I know so many nice old Winchester boys and I've never met any one who was at school with my husband. Perhaps I'm not primitive enough.'

A few days ago Naylor would have welcomed the situation, although her face was rather greasy. She was a not unattractive, embittered young woman, speaking his own language of little digs and understatements. She had done her hair in a different way and was braving her husband's unrelenting disapproval. He would stare at her coiffure silently, then manage a sort of unconscious wince, as if he was thinking of something else and only the protesting muscles of his face were aware of her. He treated Naylor with old world discourtesy.

'Well, tomorrow we shall be on the way to the aold country. Ai hev decided to gao back for a bit. Ai never hed mech use for expatriates, you knaow.'

Miserable as he was, Naylor was roused to vanquish his enemy. He thought of trying to force a battle of country seats. 'Do you know Wiltshire? What fun. It's my favourite county, though I only know the parts round Wilton and Longleat' – something, anyhow, on those lines. Just as Americans, when they meet, search frantically for a common acquaintance in a familiar city, and are delighted when they find one, so the English try to find a place they both know and then mention people that the other will, with luck, not have met, but certainly have heard of. The one nation seeks the warmth of humanity in every contact, the other tries to prove each party worthy of respect. But Naylor had a better idea. A little way up the road, walking down to keep an appointment, he saw, arm in arm, Toni and Sonia. 'Must get some cigarettes,' he murmured, and went out to intercept them. 'Hullo, are you dining with the Fosters, too?' he said. 'We've just missed them and they've left a message for us to join them in Antibes.'

'Antibes!' said Toni radiantly.

'Yes, here's a taxi, jump in.'

As the taxi went by the garden he leant far out of the window blocking the view of it from Toni and Sonia. He saw Foster rising to his feet waving furiously.

'Cannes,' he yelled out, 'Cannes.'

'Who was there?' said Toni.

'Oh, only good old Rascasse.'

Arrived at Antibes it became more difficult to deal with his precious cargo. After inquiring for Foster at the Brasserie on the square, he suggested a visit to Geraldine. They were delighted at the idea. The taxi took them along by the sea margin; a belated cicada chirred in a dusty pine; scattered uncomfortable villas gave way to broken rocks; the woods of the cape, spotted with hoardings, came down to the inhospitable beaches, filling the air with the scent of resin, and a shameless chocolate-box sunset disfigured the west. The intolerable melancholy, the dinginess, the corruption of that tainted inland sea overcame him. He felt the breath of centuries of wickedness and disillusion; how many civilizations had staled on that bright promontory! Sterile Phoenicians, commerical-minded Greeks, destructive Arabs, Catalans, Genoese, hysterical Russians, decayed English, drunken Americans, had mingled with the autochthonous gangsters – everything that was vulgar, acquisitive, piratical and decadent in capitalism had united there, crooks, gigolos, gold-diggers and captains of industry through twenty-five centuries had sprayed their cupidity and bad taste over it. As the enormous red sun sank in the purple sea (the great jakes, the tideless cloaca of the ancient world) the pathos of accumulated materialism, the Latin hopelessness seemed almost to rise up and hit him. Like Arab music, utterly plaintive, utterly cynical, the waves broke imperceptibly over the guano-coloured rocks. The road drew away into the pinewoods where a few shafts of sunlight expired on the rough bark. Without a garden or a drive, planked down among the saplings inside some straggling wire was the bungalow of Dicky and Geraldine. The front door was open and they tiptoed up the steps. Geraldine was in bed, in a frilly green jacket trimmed with swan's-down. Dicky lay half conscious on the mat, grunting in her stupor. There was broken crockery all over the floor and a table and chair were overturned. Naylor trod on a tomato.

'Good evening,' said Geraldine, 'I'm so sorry I can't get up. I cut my foot on a plate. Well, Toni, you see Dicky has decided to leave me. Your good influence is at work. We've had quite a talk about it, but soon everything will be all ready for you to move in.'

'Are you going to live here?' said Naylor.

'Yes, little Toni is going to come and take care of her old aunt. Have you got a cigarette?'

She snatched at the packet and leant back in the pillows, entirely sleek and feminine.

'We've just brought Toni round for a chat,' he improvised, 'we have to be getting back.'

'You go on in the taxi, I'll walk and meet you afterwards,' Toni answered, looking tenderly at Geraldine from the end of the bed.

They walked out over the body on the floor and got back into the taxi. It was much darker now, the velvety dust rose in little clouds under the wheels, the sea was black: unshining. Sonia stared forward, her elbows on her knees, her hands propping up her chin; a large tear rolled down her cheek.

Ariane, ma sœur, de quel amour blessée
Vous mourûtes aux bords ou vous fûtes laissée!

At this moment she must be in the act, they were both thinking, and they understood with the certainty of despair that from now on they had lost not her alone but all excuse for their ideal of her – and to whom!

Naylor also felt the unfamiliar grimaces, the atrophied ducts straining. His face puckered into the mould of grief. He dropped a tear on the fifty-franc note as he paid the taxi, and felt suddenly proud of himself. The sluices still worked. Sonia walked towards the café. Tears in women, so forbidding with familiarity, can be infinitely beautiful at first; Naylor, though aware how transitory was youthful sorrow, knew also how permanent it could feel; though but a willow in a summer shower, she thought herself a fir-tree settling down to a load of winter snow. Masterful, yet chastened, he piloted her to a seat in the bar.

The bar at Antibes was unique, for it was all English: Dickensian prints, red-faced policemen catching little boys bending, Cecil Aldin Scotch terriers, and a few orangoutang antics from the *Bystander* hung on the walls. Behind the bar, over which was a realistic coaching scene, a melancholy pock-marked barman served beer and whisky and cooked occasional steaks.

Sonia and Naylor sat in large leather chairs with between them a barrel table and a plate of soggy chips. He read the account of the first aquaplane wedding in the local paper. If there was ever an English revolution, he thought, the south of France would be full of such places with names like 'The Joint and two Veg.' where aristocratic ladies with county posteriors would serve 'black velvets' and sing *John Peel* and the Eton boating song. The barman dusted a cardboard Johnny Walker and two French motorcar salesmen rattled poker dice.

Sonia said: 'I am going home tomorrow.'

'Why?'

'My law term begins soon; it will take me several days to get to Munich.'

'How will you go?'

'Hike.'

'Do you enjoy that?'

'It's the way I came.'

'I should have thought your feet would hurt so in this weather.'

'My feet?'

'How many miles do you manage a day?'

'Oh, a hundred – sometimes two, sometimes three.'

'Then you don't walk!'

'No, why should I?'

'How do you manage?'

'I get lifts in cars.'

'Is that easy?'

'There're still plenty of people willing to help a young student.'

'But don't they try to make love to you?'

'You'd better see them try! I shouldn't tolerate it. . . .'

'But isn't it rather unfair, when they do something for you that you shouldn't do anything in return.'

'I give them the pleasure of my conversation.'

'I see.'

'Oh, I'm so worried about Toni. I wish I knew what will happen to her.'

'Did meeting her come up to what you expected?'

She reflected for some time, biting her lower lip, so that he noticed above her pale mouth the ridge of yellow down.

'Yes and no – you see in Munich I was in great difficulty. I didn't know what to believe, what to do, and when a friend of mine told me all about Toni, the adventures she had had, and showed me her picture, I felt that she was a leader for me, that if I could meet her I should learn something, like people feel who go to fortune-tellers, or talk to priests and doctors. I didn't know whether to study or to enjoy myself, to be a communist or not, to invite or reject sexual experience, you understand? Besides, I was lonely. But when I caught up with Toni I found she had changed. It was I who had to look after her, she couldn't even make her bed and she was leading everybody on and not knowing what to do, and then there was poor John and poor Rascasse and Princess Rustchuk and the colonial. I had more difficulties than I had in Munich and all Toni's as well. And she couldn't make up her mind about Spain and she hadn't any money either. You see when my friend knew her she was more independent, she did what she liked and she went where she liked. Now people and money and things matter much more. I wish we could find someone to look after her.'

'I could if she'd let me.'

'Oh, no, I don't think so. I thought of Varna.'

She propped her face in her hands again, and sat looking out on the street. Her pale hair and sunburnt arms, the sad expression on her crisp features, her thick German voice, strangely affected him: he felt, as he had always felt with her and Toni, that, however morally defective their actions might seem, he was in the presence of something noble and elegiac.

A few large drops of rain fell, out of which Toni emerged glowing. 'There you are! I've run all the way.'

They ate happily, wondering a little about the Fosters, but easily resigned to the idea that they would turn up at any moment. Naylor, though he did not know much about food, was fond of severe interrogations of head waiters, even though they ended only in eggs and chicken, and he could never get over the complete unawareness of everyone in Trou of any standard of quality. Food was something they either had enough of, or didn't, and they were always embarrassed when there was a choice in the menu. As the two girls gulped down their indifferent soup or crunched pieces of stale wet lettuce he felt as if he was feeding rabbits: animals who automatically left their burrows in the evening when they heard the clink of his pail.

Unable to begin his shaky intellectual banter while they were so busy eating, he was forced to contemplate them in silence. Alas, how miserable their good looks made him! The pain of watching beautiful young girls, the isolation of desire! They reminded him of the figures in one of those pictures by Watteau that are instinct with the beauty of the moment, the fugitive distress of hedonism, the sadness that falls like a dew from pleasure, as they stand, fixed in a movement of the dance, beneath the elms, beneath the garlanded urn. It was better to be unhappy about Tahiti, to regret her obvious loss rather than to undergo this wild indefinable pain. After the meal Sonia waited while Toni took him off to look for the Fosters in the other cafés.

'They must have meant somewhere else.'

'It's so long since I've seen you,' Naylor said. 'Tell me about yourself. Are you in love with Geraldine?'

'Yes, terribly, Don't you like her?'

'Well, I hardly know her.'

'People say such awful things about her and nothing of them is true, nothing.'

'What about Princess Rustchuk now? Is she out of it?'

'Oh, how could you say so! I shall always be devoted to her – but, after all, she made me unhappy for two years. I think I owe myself a little happiness – and Geraldine so much more needs someone to look after her.'

'Are you going to live with her now Dicky's gone?'

'Well, you see, it is so difficult. I should like to, but Geraldine has lost her money, and, of course, Dicky is terrible when she gets D.T.'s but she has got enough money to give Geraldine what she's used to. Oh, it is miserable. I ask so little, you understand? I want only enough money to stay with her. I don't want to interfere with anybody. Politics, families, people, places, they mean nothing to me. I ask nothing of the world but to be left alone. Why shouldn't I have enough money to stay with the person I love?'

As they walked on past the empty cafés in the rain, Toni fretting and stamping as was her way, he noticed again what had struck him when he first saw her, the extraordinary maturity of her personality, that pagan aura which, like a verse of Meleager, surrounded the girl of nineteen with the poise and distress of the ancient world, marking her out as a being dedicated to its simple and limited cycle of joy and sorrow.

As usual, he was grateful for her confidences, while a little uneasy at their meaning. Was he expected to finance the new liaison, or was it the genuine cry of someone whose currency is the emotions, who is now made to realize the importance of ordinary lucre? He was unable to decide, for on returning to the café Sonia jumped up and, muttering something about John Foster in German, hurried Toni off to a bus. He saw them sitting next the driver, turning up each other's coat collars, while the car lurched off to Trou through the autumn rain.

VII

HE paid for the cheapest dinner he had so far given, and went back by taxi to his hotel. The thought of Tahiti was more than ever painful, yet he was the more unhappy to find the physical recollection of her less present to help him; the traces of her scent on the pillow, the animal feeling of having loved and been loved were there no longer. There had been a moment when she had leant over him, on her elbow: 'Are you dead? Are you dead? Have I killed you?' Like the circles made by a stone in a pond, his memories of her, yesterday so close and finite, widened into larger, hazier ripples that troubled every part of his

97

consciousness instead of his limbs alone. When he could not sleep, he got up and packed, and was glad to think he need not spend another night in the room he had shared with her. He paid his bill the next morning and put his luggage on to the bus. It set him down by the little hotel in Trou where – it seemed in some former existence – he had stopped till his moment of deafness passed. The people were glad to see him, for several of his hospitalities had taken place in their café or their garden, and he went upstairs to his bare room where the iron bedstead shimmered under the mosquito net, with a sensation of homecoming. The window looked away from the little garden and the street where the buses rattled on their way to Nice, so that he was unable to watch the troglodytes descend the hill for their aperitive. He supposed that a real investigator would have paid the extra rent for a front room, like those detectives who take whole floors in hotels so as to be near the crucial keyhole, but he was content with his view of white walls, washing on the line, and a glimpse beyond of reedy meadows. He knew that the inn, besides being opposite a bus stop, was the place where most of the hill-dwellers went for their letters, and where those who were not accredited to either of the private bathrooms, Foster's, or the Corsican's, came down to wash. When he had unpacked he began a letter to Tahiti, a letter which was to remind her of their ecstasy, in which he quoted Milton about their

> . . . joies
> Then sweet, now sad to mention, through dire change
> Befallen us unforeseen. . . .

After this he was able to go off to lunch. It was over his loyal reading of the *Daily Mail* with his coffee, while he was devouring an article on colibacillosis, a disease whose symptoms were applicable to almost every human condition, and which was practically incurable, that he noticed a procession coming down the hill. There were Foster and Mrs Foster, Toni, Sonia, and Rascasse, and one or two Poles and Germans whom he did not know. The Fosters looked straight past him, and Rascasse demurely kept his eyes to the ground. From his table in the corner of the garden, he was able to get a clear view of the antique frieze. It was more important for him than he realized, for he was watching the leave-taking of Sonia, the first of the hill-dwellers to hesitate, like a swallow on the Provençal telegraph wires, and then take wing. It was a damp afternoon, and various pink and purple drinks were brought out to them. Then the moment came. Foster strapped on her enormous rucksack, Toni hugged, Rascasse kissed her. Lola, who had joined them, screamed banalities, everybody waved, and Sonia, the tears streaming from her eyes, set off with long strides down the road.

Naylor also was uncomfortably moved. He held the newspaper up and read furiously – 'Constipation and diarrhoea alternate or in many cases co-exist. The sufferer wakes up in the morning as tired as when he goes to bed, and complains frequently of fatigue, headache, and pains in the back. A rigid diet, the total forswearing of game, rich meat, sugar, cream, starch, and such delicacies as foie gras or crab and lobster, combined with strict teetotalism may eventually purify the stomach to an extent which will prevent the bacilli from multiplying, but hope must never be held out of a complete cure. It is a disease which increases as the body's resistance to it is diminished, and in many cases . . .' He heard a step on the other side of the newspaper and lowered it to find Rascasse in front of him, his large meek eyes were also brimming. The men of Trou, in fact, could weep like Elizabethans or, if necessary, Homeric heroes.

'Well, she's gone,' he said, and Naylor thought he had

never looked more Jewish, more fatalistic and pogrom-conscious. It was the lack of hope in their lives, he realized, that accounted for the impression of aged, vanishing civilizations that hung over Trou; Rascasse, so boisterous, yet so patient, and resigned to adversity, recalled the Jews of the captivity; Toni, Sonia, and the others brought into modern life the despondency of the pagan world. It was like going for a walk in a London suburb, among the arterial roads, ribbon developments, and petrol stations and coming, in some hollow, upon a decayed eighteenth-century manor, Canons or Osterley, that take one disturbingly with the chill of the past.

'Anyhow, you have your picture of her,' answered Naylor, thinking of the little portrait on wood he had seen. Remembering how exquisitely it was done, the white shirt and the whites of her large eyes contrasting with the sombre background and the golden yellow of her skin and hair, it came suddenly to him how much Rascasse must be in love with her and with what deep and genuine devotion. 'I haven't even a photograph of Tahiti,' he continued, 'and you at least know that the person you love likes you and is separated inevitably from you, while I may see Tahiti pass at any moment, and be cut by her.'

'Oh, by the bye,' said Rascasse, 'I saw her last night and said how unhappy you were about her leaving you.'

'And what did she say?'

'She said: "Well, what else does he expect for a pair of shoes?" '

'Thank you.'

'Anyhow, you lazy bum, it doesn't look as if we'll have that walk to La Gaude. I'm off myself tonight, remember, and the next thing you'll hear about me is a card for my vernissage. *L'exposition Rascasse! Tout le monde viendra.* I shouldn't be surprised if there weren't counts and barons and *Monsieur le Vicomte de Noailles*. There's a guy that could be of use to me! Yes, Sir! *Il y aura le tout Paris* and a write-up in the *Tribune* as well.'

'And then what?'

'Then I shall be famous and rich and get my own back on those lousy fairies who are always sneering at me, gloating over my poverty, you understand? And I shall go and propose to my adorable little Sonia and everything will be jay – and by the bye, thanks a lot for spoiling my last evening with her, sneaking her off to dinner like that – that was a nice thing to do, oh, yes, a very friendly act, just because Rascasse is poor, because he hasn't any money, you think it fun to humiliate him publicly to show how a few filthy francs can get his girl away when he needs her most, when a tried friend, a gentleman like Foster, a man of ancient lineage, gives a farewell dinner for him and his girl. You, you whom he introduced to everyone in the town, whose social entry he sponsored, helping you to meet the regular fellows instead of all the bums, you retaliate by basely undermining him, you understand, by behaving with reckless and cynical ingratitude like any of the other lousy people in this hole!'

'Well, really, I'm very sorry. I simply wanted to annoy Foster in return for a piece of unpardonable rudeness, by taking Toni out to dinner. I had no intention of interfering with your plans.'

'Well, well, I forgive you. You know it is a funny thing, however cross he gets, a Jew can never look angry with his eyes. Have you noticed? I don't believe you meant it, but it is your beastly cynicism, Naylor, that gets you into trouble, and as Foster says, all cynicism is so damned sentimental. No wonder you put people's backs up; and let me give you one word of advice. You're broke. All right; plenty of fine chaps have been broke before. But don't put on airs about it. I speak as your friend, see; well, there's plenty of weathercocks in a hole like this, and don't be surprised if you get a bit less consideration from certain people whom I shall not name: if you find people less inclined to fall in with all your wishes than formerly. That's the way of the world, my friend. Well, I'll be seeing you before I go this evening.'

Naylor went back to his room and lay down. Was he cynical? Is it cynical to learn from much unpleasant experience that experience is usually unpleasant; to believe, as Santayana puts it, that life is not a feast or a spectacle, but a predicament; and, if this is cynical, why then is it sentimental? Was Voltaire or Bismarck sentimental? The phrase of Foster's was one of those sloppy half-truths; but, as is usual with them, it was the nastier half. All that followed was that the habit and profession of cynicism can often exist without the requisite gold reserves of emotion to back them; in which case, they become as sentimental as the habit of optimism. To expect the worst from people and events is to enjoy delicious surprises; to expect the best is to receive disappointments. Human life was a tragedy, he thought, redeemed by the most exquisite consolations. But still a tragedy. What he felt was that he and Toni and even Rascasse were 'old souls', people who beneath their high spirits concealed a fundamental and Asiatic despair, whose only religious belief was in the Jealous God, the Envious Being who would pinch any happiness that came one's way, if one showed it, or destroy any excellence as surely as he grudged Toni her beauty, Sonia her virginity, or Naylor his thousand a year. Compared to such fatalism, the ordinary cynic was a Bedales girl. It was the uncynical moments, perhaps, of cynical people that were sentimental, the discovery of the prostitute with a soul, the lily on the dung-heap. In any case he was not wholly cynical, he reflected, simply rather soured by the difficulties of obtaining his need of sexual gratification, and because, having a little money, he hoped to buy genuine affection with it. His income was really the cause of all his troubles; it put him on his guard with the world and gave him the pretensions without which he would never have dared to demand so much from life. Since he always expected his money to purchase happiness, he was really an optimist, and that was why he had so many disillusions. The higher the head, the harder it strikes the ground. If only he could disregard money in his dealings with people, if only he could be less suspicious! Perhaps he would learn that lesson too, now he was broke. Then Trou would have meant something. Otherwise, more unpleasantness. We all find faults, but those who look for gratitude find the ugliest.

It was extraordinary that, whenever he tried to take a siesta, his thoughts were always so depressing. Perhaps the small hours of the afternoon were in affinity with those of the night and released similar bogeys. Money. Tahiti. Unpopularity. Sex. Sex. Tahiti. Unpopularity. Money.

Instead, he went out for a walk; the landscape was settling into autumn, the clouds returned after the rain, the air was wet and stagnant. He passed a garden where a clump of bananas spread their large melancholy fronds against a wall. The deep penetrating green against the dark sky was significant and oppressive. Behind them stood a neat trim house from whose shuttered window came a few screams, followed by a man's angry voice and a woman's sobbing. He edged a little nearer the shutters, but at that moment they were flung open. In the aperture he caught a glimpse of Lola, the blood streaming from her mouth, pointing hysterically at him, and, over her shoulder, the Corsican's handsome face suffused with rage. The windows slammed immediately. He broke into a run. When he got back to the hotel there was a familiar commotion. He retired to his seat in the garden like a hunter watching a water-hole, confident that whatever happened in the village would happen here. This time it was the Fosters leaving; they were on their way to catch a boat back to England from Marseilles. They sat round the table with Toni and Rascasse and Sonia's colonial as their entourage; they did not wave to him but he saw Foster's round varsity face continually turning in his direction. He ordered a Pernod and then another, hardly realizing that for the first time he was drinking heavily by himself. After the second, he began to brood about Tahiti and decided to go and beard her in her hotel. He would walk right up to her, even if she was surrounded by those awful men, simply dominate, standing over her in silence, with a magnificent reproachful look. She would rise and, without a word spoken, follow him. One more Pernod and he'd go. Sitting muttering to himself in his corner, he was not very conscious of the Fosters' departure; nor was he interrupted till Rascasse came to say good-bye to him. 'Aren't you coming to the station, you lazy bum? It's going to be a swell send-off.'

'Station?'

'Sure, don't you want to say good-bye to Lola? She's going straight down there. Everybody's going to be there, Toni, Jimmy, the Corsicans; it'll be a swell party.'

'No, no, you go instead.'

'Oh, so that's how you feel! Well, there are a lot of little things I've got to see about. Maybe we'll meet in Paris. I'll send you a card for my exhibition. Remember your picture's going to be the best thing in it – yours and the Corsican's and his wife's and Sonia's and Foster's. Yes, sir, Rascasse is going to be famous. By the way, don't forget you still have to pay me a hundred francs.'

Naylor rose unsteadily. 'Good-bye, good-bye, Rascasse. Now that you're going I should like to take the opportunity of telling you that you are the biggest sponge, the biggest bore, though neither of the words is probably familiar to you since they imply the existence of their opposites, that I have ever, ever, ever. . . .'

He sat down again. Rascasse beamed. He was busy taking down from the bar the picture which had first attracted Naylor's attention.

'Oh, that's O.K. Just forget about it. You must come and have dinner with me when you get to Paris.'

'Thank you. That would be a unique experience.'

'Good old Naylor. We've had some wonderful times together, eh?'

'I imagine you are speaking for yourself.'

'Gee, that's good. I appreciate wonderfully an idiomatic terminology – still, Rascasse speaks pretty good English. Don't you think I'd get by in England with it? Say, that's an idea. Why shouldn't I come to England after my exhibition in Paris? Then it'll be your turn to introduce *me* to some useful people. Maybe I'll get some commissions and have another exhibition there! How's that for an idea? Do you know this guy Clive Bell, the critic?'

'I have met him.'

'Splendid. It seems a pity I have to go to Paris at all. Why not let's all go straight to England and you'll give a party for me and Lola.'

'Yes, why not, but, on the other hand, why?'

'Why, because you know influential people, because it will make you famous; besides, we're pals, aren't we?'

'Are we?'

'Sure. Still worrying about Sonia? Oh, I'm not sore any longer about that, I've forgiven you. Forget it. But this England scheme; now that's something, eh!'

'It's a grand idea, but I happen to have very little money.'

'Well, later in the year then, and here's a piece of advice, Naylor. Never let on you're broke to anyone – see – anyone. It may be the fashion in England, but over here, *c'est une chose qui ne se fait pas.*' He patted him on the back, gathered up his canvases, kissed the waitress, and made off towards the station. Naylor nodded his head in a few sharp jerks and climbed up to his room, taking the Pernod bottle.

This was the beginning of the end. Henceforward every day was to bring a new departure. The Rock Pool seemed to be slowly drained of all aquatic life while Naylor, as his bill mounted and mounted at the hotel, was being gradually tangled up in a skein of small financial obligations. He passed the time in a Pernod haze, not very often leaving his room, and brooding miserably over Tahiti. Sometimes the alcohol, like a supercharger, would drive him into brief spells of violent energy, and he would start off to walk or run to Cannes, determined to drag Tahiti back by the hair; at others he would indulge in voluptuous daydreams, lying on the iron bed under the netting. She would come straight in without a knock, radiant and smiling. 'Did you think I was never coming back!' – 'Darling.' Or perhaps she would simply lie down beside him and say nothing at all. She would wear the same stiff white canvas shorts, the same bandage round her knee, her large firm swelling breasts taut under the linen shirt, her chestnut hair tousled, her blue eyes laughing, her lips open to show her dazzling Polynesian teeth. 'Oh, I've been so unhappy', she might begin.

VIII

HIS days began to fit themselves to the discipline of solitary drinking – he was asleep most of the morning, usually rising after lunch, which seemed to him a superfluous meal. At some time in the afternoon he would get up and attend to the business of the day. First a Fernet Branca, some strong coffee, and a hair, or rather a tuft, of the dog

that bit him. Then a walk down the street to the barber's
for a shave, and to the *tabac* for some cigarettes and the
newspaper. He would return to the hotel garden and sit
frowning over the news. This was his soberest moment,
and he was fond of convincing himself that he was a not
unimportant cog in the machine. He would shake his head
and flick his fingers. 'Yes, yes, H'm. I was afraid of that,' he
would mutter as if each issue of the *Continental Daily
Mail* were an agonized dispatch-rider, imploring him to be
told what answer to take back. He played *Dans les steppes
de l'Asie Centrale* continuously on the gramophone, and
pored over a pompous and spooky surrealist magazine.
Several young poets described their extraordinary experience. Walking down the rue de Rennes they felt a wave
of antipathy from an optician's shop. A., B., C., D., sub-
stantiated the phenomenon. They traced the hostility to a
tray of glass eyes where they observed, reflected in each
pupil, the railway station at Laroche-Migennes. B. finally
entered the shop but was overcome by malease. C. found
the optician himself more *significantly* obscene than he
had conceived possible any tactile object. 'A bishop', D.
described him, 'who, beneath his surplice, sports a can-can
dancer's frou-frous.' Behind the tray of eyes was a coloured
post-card, of the purest integrity, depicting the tomb of
Chateaubriand at Saint-Malo. All were seized by the com-
punction to go there on the first train, and on arrival felt
'an animosity not to be endured: pricking of the eyes and
thumbs, and overwhelming sense of despair, schizo-
phrenia, and costive headache'. Four out of six in a ques-
tionnaire to 'What time is it?' replied: 'Morning'. Three
out of five, and one abstention to the query 'Where would
you urinate?', answered: 'I would retain my urine', and
three out of six, being asked to describe what utensil or
appliance doing what to what the statue suggested, replied: 'The very small, the very violet mandibles of a slug

or other malcological specimen closing inexorably round a brass lathe which rotates rapidly images (1) of the Sacré-Cœur at Montmartre (2) of the tertiary erotic zone of a deputy, and (3) of Montmartre with the Sacré-Cœur'.

Sometimes he procured instead the highbrow weeklies, and to their superior whining added his own grave apprehension. This done, he began on the Pernods, and his plans for Tahiti. At first, self-pity would predominate, then his grievance would crystallize into demands for action. He would send the waiter off to telephone, ask for pen and paper and telegraph forms, sometimes for a time-table. The staff of the hotel, to whom his mode of life seemed as sensible as any other, and, indeed, one to which they were well accustomed, would bring them to him, while the preparations for his dinner went on uninter-rupted. He dined in the dingy restaurant, where his table-cloth, with its coffee and wine-stains, was the only one set. Nondescript soup, fish, evidently from some further ocean, meat that was already slightly balkanized, and a few dried figs with rotten almonds in a basket formed his meal, which he washed down with lilac carafes of wine. Afterwards, he would have a few brandies in the café and go up to bed with the Pernod bottle. He paid his bill conscientiously at first, remembering Rascasse's advice. The weather was uniformly wet, the rain fell continuously, as if the two months between the seasons was being used by Nature for the annual hosing of her favourite playground. The sea was calm under the downpour, the plane trees peeled and yellowed. Cars and horses skidded on the tram-lines. The streets filled up with mud. The gutters of the hill-town sluiced over and no one wore sandals any more or went down to bathe. The few remain-ing inhabitants were apparently house-bound; Toni was all the time at Antibes, Eddie was still in hospital, and the Corsican had gone back to Ajaccio to cook an election.

Only once had he seen Tahiti, driving slowly through the rain on the road to Cannes with Jimmy in a borrowed roadster. He had got bored with his hair, which, still platinum at the ends, had now a black fuzz growing underneath it and was exactly parti-coloured like a tapir's. Tahiti, in spite of the letters and telegrams he constantly sent her, did not merely cut him, but gave him a look full of intelligent curiosity, as if he were a local celebrity. Once Jimmy came in very drunk and stood for a moment beside him. 'Well, how's the lion-tamer? I hear you're broke, old chap.'

'Yes, I am.'

'Would a couple of hundred dollars be any use?'

'Why, yes, it would make all the difference in the world.'

Jimmy leant over, giving him back a breath as bad as his own. 'Well, good-bye, you madcap, see you in Carpathian Ruthenia. I haven't got a cent.'

Another time, Varna came into the bar. The Bastion had been closed for several days. He put on what he hoped was a social manner on her arrival, but only managed a leer so savage that she stood a few yards away from his table.

'Why, Varna, this is a pleasure. How are you? What have you been doing? Come and sit down a moment.'

'No, thank you very much, I have to fly.'

'To fly? That's very interesting. Come and tell me all about it.'

'I can't. I'm so busy packing.'

'Don't say you're leaving too. I can't bear it.'

'I'm motoring to Paris tomorrow.'

'With Duff – how nice for you.'

'No, Duff's going off to stay with some relations along the coast. I'm taking little Toni along. She wants to get a job in a bookshop, somewhere where her languages would come in useful.'

'Is she living at Geraldine's now?'

'No, there's no room, because of Dicky's nurses. She's living at the haunted house.'

'Which is that?'

'Along the road, near the bridge. You must have passed it.'

'I'll go and say good-bye to her.'

'I'm sure she'd love it.'

'And dear, dear Duff. I must go and say goodbye to her too.'

'I'll take any message.'

'Humm – I see.'

It was meant to be cordial, but the result was a sinister falsetto wheeze that sent her backing.

'Hey! Hey! Wait a minute.'

She waved and hurried out. He got up, knocking over a chair. They always seemed particularly badly placed. Too late to catch up with her. He set out for the haunted house. It was about half a mile along the road, beyond the railway station and the 'Rendez-vous des Boulomanes', just within walking distance, a pink rambling building in a quincunx of nibbled palms. A few bills had been posted on the end walls, and were now peeling in the rain. The walls inside had been whitewashed and were scribbled with primitive obscenities, and a little way from the broken shutters, the buses careered up and down. He remembered hearing that some African troops had been quartered there, but were evacuated, owing to the superstitious terror which the house inspired. He could find no evidence of later habitation. Evidently Varna was believing what Toni wished her to believe. Living chiefly in his bedroom, he saw the world, on these rare sorties, with accumulated precision. The scene seemed an epitome of the whole region, the old decaying house plastered with liquor advertisements, the palms vainly struggling to appear indigenous, the lorries and buses, the fringe of gimcrack villas, and beyond them the great white bed of the Var through which, as a thread in the centre, the granite subalpine torrent flowed by its poplars and reed-beds to end in a golf-course. The twilight was falling as he returned. From the lighted doorways came the smell of frying olive oil; everything was brown and humid. He walked slowly with his hands spread out, taking the pulse of the time and the place, his lean figure inserted in the night like a thermometer. For once he was sober enough to feel lonely and decided to go to Nice after dinner. It was ages since he had had any city life, and he longed for bands and brasseries and something stupid and cosy, like a 'house' or a French comic song. He drank little with his meal, and jumped into a bus. The wide crescent of the esplanade swung into sight. The rain was over for a little, and an icy wind from the Alps swept down the boulevards. He bought a few illustrated magazines and settled down on the Place Masséna. It was a moment of freedom, like the end of a play in which, at school, he had had to say the last words: 'and thingummy's his own man again'. He lit a cigar, and surveyed the crowded brasserie over a double brandy. It was a relief to see the sexes differentiated in the good old urban way and trousers on the proper legs; but how ugly they all were. City dwellers have grown so used to being undersized, anæmic and plain that it was only possible after an absence to notice how all charm of appearance had totally atrophied; how the men looked like beetles and the women like bugs. What beauty remained was clearly professional. Still, they were normal people; they loved, if at all, with orthodoxy, and they paid their share. A band in a corner churned out a kind of grown-up's bedtime music. The waiters hurried backwards and forwards, a hundred café crèmes steamed on the marble tables, a hundred off-the-peg bottoms squatted on the plush. Supposing he enjoyed himself that evening, then offered to pay half the petrol if Varna took him up

north in the car with her? He could still settle his hotel bill
by cheque. Back to the herd again was his slogan, and that
would be the cheapest way to do it. She was his last chance
of escape. Besides, he would see a lot of Toni. There would
be the Rhône valley, the magnificent restaurants of Bur-
gundy, then Paris with the braziers on the terraces, while
standing with her beneath the catalpas of the Place de
Furstemberg, or on the Pont des Arts, he would show her
the most civilized view in the world. Thinking of Toni, he
remembered Maxim's and decided to look in for a moment; after that he would go to a 'house' – not one like that
of Trou, where there were only three girls, two of whom
had posed for Renoir, but one that was run on an æsthetic
rather than an antiquarian basis. He thought with pleasure
of the time-honoured ceremonial. The dark street with the
big numbers, the trilling of the bell – still time to flee – the
stern mothers-superior who arranged the business side of
things. Even then it was not too late to back out. And the
ominous jingle of the mechanical piano, the row of staring
girls, giggling in their shifts or balancing in stiff uneasy
poses on blocks of wood! *'Alors, monsieur, vous avez
choisi? Vous voulez monter avec la petite?'* It was a rite as
solemn as the burial service, a sacrament in which he
re-stated his guilt, the helpless trend of all his actions back
to the slime of original sin. 'O Lord, for as much as we have
no power in ourselves to help ourselves.' And then, too,
there was the ritual of choosing, under the stern task-
mistress's eye, to the strains of some desultory tango, a
guilty companion, someone to drag down with him, someone who was paid to be pleasant and in whose embraces he
could drown, at the moment of supremacy, all that strange
world of women's beauty, so wild, so heart-rending and
unobtainable. Sunk, like Lyonesse, the bells of their
dominion might still seem to ring on stormy nights, the
city under the sea be visible through the green calms, but

soon it would be but a fable; and so he affirmed, with each visit, the emptiness of sexual experience, the banality of love. But Maxim's first – Jimmy's delicious night-box – and he entered the gaudy portals already tingling with a preliminary feeling of wickedness. If only the dons and the ushers could see him now, he'd show the old toss-pots! He stalked to a table, still adequately Byronic, but when two women sat down at it, his native indecision began to operate and he smiled weakly at them, while indicating that they should go. They recognized his type with pleasure – the young man who longs to speak and is frightened of being spoken to – and soon were pouting for cigarettes, drinking champagne and making the paper sheaths in which the straws were served shoot out from his nostrils.

When he insisted they should leave with him, they explained that the management did not allow them to go till five o'clock.

'You might have told me before.'

'*Qu'est-ce qu'il dit, le jeune anglais? Ce n'est pas la façon de parler à une petite dame.*'

The wretched farce proceeded; older than Sumer, the role of sucker was played out to the end. He escaped three hundred francs to the bad, the equivalent of two women and an indecent cinema. In the square, an individual separated from the cab-rank and heaved towards him. '*Eh, bé, alors, C'est lui le voleur, le sale anglais.*' His short arms hanging down like a bear's he towered over, thrusting his fist under Naylor's nose – '*Eh, bé! Ça vous dit quelque chose? Ça, c'est la même en toutes les langues, eh? Ça vous fait comprendre ce que c'est d'être un voleur, un escroc, eh?*'

'*Mais, monsieur, c'est une erreur, je ne vous connais pas.*'

The man hit him hard in the mouth. '*Salaud!*' he roared. '*Sale métèque, sale boche, une contravention, le violon*

*pour lui, va t'en te faire enculer, cochon d'américain —
encore un qui veut se sauver à l'anglaise — espèce de
sénateur.'*

He went to the police station, with its relative quiet, and
heard the charge against him. He owed the taxi-driver
three hundred francs for keeping him waiting all night
after that first evening at Maxim's, a hundred francs for the
work he lost in consequence, and a mysterious hundred to
police charities, to show his gratitude for escaping a night
in gaol. His mouth bled, the gendarmes stood guard, the
taxi-driver related his grievances to the angry mob. It could
have happened anywhere. He knew all the helplessness of
any foreigner who contravenes any law. At one time, he
had believed in the superannuated doctrine of *civis roma-
nus sum*, that English and Americans received the benefit
of the doubt in their disputes with waiters and drunken
aborgines. After that creed was exploded, there still remained a belief in the efficacy of his country's representa-
tives; but a dispute over a bill in Lisbon had removed it. He
had been able to procure the service of an Honarary
Attaché, a milky young man who was in trouble because,
being told to 'return the calls' of a series of Spanish visi-
tors, he had taken their cards from the tray and driven
round, putting them back in the houses from which they
had originated. He was in consequence only too glad of a
chance to make himself unpleasant, and treated Naylor to
a lecture; since when he had come to understand the true
diplomat's horror of getting into any situation where he
could possibly be of use to his compatriots, and consequently lose 'face'. He distributed the remaining five hundred francs of his pocket-money; but since he had come
out without his passport it was thought better he should
remain in custody all the same.

IX

THE next day, when he got back, it was to another kind of prison. He now had fifty francs in currency, and credit at the hotel – he could get meals, drink, cigarettes and newspapers there, but nothing anywhere else. He had enough money in the bank to dish out small advances to the proprietors, but not enough to pay his bill and go away. The weather continued melancholy and dull, the sky was a spittoon full of small phlegm-coloured clouds. He went to bed as soon as he got back and woke up in the evening. Below in the garden was the same disturbance which always occasioned in him a wave of sadness and curiosity. From the bathroom window, where he was dressing his wounds, he looked down at Varna, Duff, Toni, and the apache woman standing round a small car. They were tying luggage on the running boards, fussing about and misdirecting each other, so that he perceived how much more feminine were the most masculine of women than the most feminine of men. He saw Duff leave the group and enter the hotel and suddenly heard her behind him. 'Why, it's you!' she said. 'They told me there was some string in the bathroom. I thought you'd left long ago.'

'No, but I expect to be going in a day or two.'

'It's too bad; you should have gone with Varna; she was trying everywhere to get a passenger who'd pay some of the petrol.'

'Why didn't she ask me, then?'

'Oh, I expect she was afraid it wouldn't be grand enough.'

'It's grand enough for Baroness von Schaan.'

'Who? – Oh, for Toni; well, she's very lucky to be going. She very nearly didn't take her.'

'Why not?'

'Why, when she was invited she went round telling everyone how terrible it would be for me, and who was going to break the news? And what would become of me without Varna? And did they think she should refuse to go with her? The whole town has been round condoling, and asking what we quarrelled about, and how long the affair between Varna and Toni has been going on.'

'So what has happened?'

'Well, Varna went and told Toni that she was only taking her to Paris because Sonia asked her to, before she left, and that, if she said another word about herself or me, she could stay behind and see what it was like trying to please Geraldine without any money, and Toni cried a great deal and said how wicked everybody was, and then she giggled and said: "Dear Varna, you don't have to tell me that, I won't give you away", and Varna got mad and gave her a good old-fashioned spanking, and since then she's been perfectly sweet.'

'Of course, I've always thought you and Varna the only decent people around here. I should like you to know it before you go.'

'Oh, thanks very much, she'll be pleased. I'll tell her.'

She blushed a little. Pale, distinguished, slightly awkward, she was one of those calm, dreamy, flat-chested blondes whose very absence of sex provokes it in others, and whose lack of vulgarity is their most definite quality.

He took a gentle hold of her elbow and gave her a 'magnetic' look. 'Dear Duff, I shall miss you. I shall miss you terribly. Do you remember how we first met. I shall always see your dishevelled nordic head bent over the solitaire cards. You know, you're very attractive.' He tightened his grip. 'You're so alluring, so cerebral. I should like to kiss you. May I? Please?'

'No. Let go.'

'What a way to talk!' He managed a laugh, if that was the right name for his lubricious whinny.

She stood the same height as he, a grave and harmless American on whom it would be quite safe to practise. 'Darling!'

It was, to do the place justice, the first time he had had his face slapped in Trou. She walked out in a cold rage. He stopped to bathe the cut in his lip which she had reopened. Did they perhaps all call him the lion-tamer, or only that horrible Jimmy? The noise of the motor drew him to the window again. Varna was now at the wheel. Duff was inspecting the straps, the apache lady was knocking her pipe out on the luggage grid. 'Your navvy friend,' he thought.

Toni came round from the other side. He had never seen her in skirts before. She wore a dark flannel suit, very loosely cut, but even so it revealed an exquisite curve of the hips, an unexpectedly graceful line that her usual shorts and sailor's trousers had never suggested. Varna wore a short-skirted suit and a tie. It was curious, he thought, how women of her type stuck to the fashion of the early 'twenties. Her regulation uniform suggested the war work, the Eton crops and long cigarette holders of the Radclyffe Hall period. Just as Edwardian beaux, and a few queens and other great ladies, maintained the fashions of the nineteen hundreds, so perhaps do we all try unconsciously to preserve the plumage in which the world has first found us desirable. Toni stood with one foot on the running board like a figure on a Greek vase, her skirt falling peplum-wise in pleats from her bent knee, her hands raised to the hood above her straight shoulders; he studied her pose, *libertina fretis acrior*, for it was the last time he would see her. Then she got in and took her place beside Varna. The car drove off, the others walked up the hill; he caught a glimpse of her face framed in the window like a small nectarine, then it was gone.

He went back to the Pernod régime. It was extraordinary how everything stank of it. All his clothes, the walls, the bed seemed soused in the aniseed odour. He felt things snapping in his head, strange combustions went on behind his eyes, when he closed them; incredibly evil faces, old men with knobs and wens, Goya witches, bestial animals, appeared and reappeared. His hand was too shaky to read; anyhow, he hadn't got any books. He began to talk to himself, arguing with Tahiti or Rascasse, refusing to get Duff out of a hole, insulting Jimmy and Eddie-from-the-top. Occasionally he tried to write a letter. *'Monsieur le Ministre de Justice, j'ai à vous raconter une terrible perversion de justice qui est arrivée à un jeune anglais, homme d'affaires et écrivain connu, à Trou-sur-Mer, département des Alpes-Maritimes. Il s'agit d'un taxi.'* To the British Consul at Nice: 'Sir, I wish to draw your attention to a flagrant miscarriage of justice'.

The waiter usually picked the sheets up after he went back to bed, but often he let them blow away. On some evenings, the weather was finer and the sea was pulled over the beach like an eiderdown. On others, the mistral blew for three, nine, or twelve days and everything was foamy: the sea was blue and green instead of oyster-coloured; the sky was further and the mountains nearer; he could see the yellow houses of Saint-Pierre and La Gaude. Those days his head hurt him most, for the wind turned his corner glacial and dusty. In the street, the plane trees rocked and shed their leaves, then, when the wind was over, he would walk out to the haunted house and sit on the bench among the palms and the sodden grass. It was usually too muddy to go up the hill into Trou; nobody was left there; even the unfrocked priest had joined the Orthodox Church and been put in charge of a Russian monastery in the mountains, and the colonial had gone to Vichy for his liver trouble. Both the bars were closed. It seemed Eddie wouldn't be out of hospital for a long while and the only time he walked up to the top he was depressed by the cactus and bamboos on the side of the hill, for he associated their leaden greenness with remorse and imperfection; the sad feathery shafts dripping rain, intense against the dark sky, suggested paradise lost and emphasized the loneliness which had become his element.

It was about this time a year ago that in his researches into Rogers he had discovered Holland House. Opposite an amusement palace, with a few slot machines and a shooting gallery, he had found the great iron gates open and walked up the drive. The leaves had not been swept; the fine melancholy avenue wound away from the traffic into those fields and copses of Lord Ilchester's where the pheasants still rocketed and the nightingales still sang. He had not been able, in his trespassing, to find the bench beloved by the author of the *Pleasures of Memory* engraved by his friend with a couplet so much better than any of his own:

> Here Rogers sate, and here for ever dwell
> With me those pleasures that he sang so well.

This house, in fact, had been the most sacred thing in his life, and he remembered that the Banker Bard couldn't talk ten minutes without expressing his gratitude to the family of Fox. Beyond the lawns with their smell of wood-smoke where he dared not venture, he saw the huge gabled Jacobean pile and, rising out of the walled garden in the autumn mist, the famous cedars. Somewhere inside was the library where Addison had paced and Fox sought among the books for those virtues of freedom and rapidity which he relished. There Allen, Smith, and Luttrell had joked and philosophized, Lady Holland commanded, and Macaulay obeyed; there Rogers's apartment had been perpetually ready, and Lord Holland, his disarming benevolence masking a central aristocratic coldness, had illumined, like an old moon, the decline of the Whigs and of the age of reason and idiosyncrasy, far into the raw Victorian day.

Emerging from his reverie he noticed he was passing by a door which seemed vaguely familiar. Above it was painted 'Villa Kuplablox'; the monotonous rise and fall of someone practising scales was audible, then the keyboard was silent, and the door flung open.

'Why, hullo! Welcome, stranger. How nice of you to come up to see me. Come in, won't you, if you don't mind the frightful mess everything's in, but I haven't been at all well, and haven't been able to go out and get anything done for days.'

It was Ruby, whom he hadn't seen since the episode after the party. He wasn't sure if she remembered him or not; such a greeting, in Trou, was simply a social formula.

When he got inside, he was at once bowled over by the familiar reek of Pernod. The room might have been his own.

'What does the name on your house mean?'

'Why we christened it that because it's a couple of blocks from the wine shop. It seemed such a hell of a long way.'

'Oh, of course, you're married, aren't you?'

'Yes, and divorced, thank you. Have a drink or would you rather have some tea?'

'A drink, if you please.'

'O.K., if you don't mind Pernod; it's all I've got at the moment. Well, it was mighty nice of you to come and call on little Ruby. It's pretty lonely up here.'

'Why do you stay, then?'

'Oh, I guess I'm kind of used to it. Why do you?'

'I find I can work here.'

'So do I. One's got to have solitude to pursue one's art, not only for the mere labour, but for the composition – that's my speciality. Have another, won't you? Of course my family would go plumb crazy if they knew the way I lived here. They simply wouldn't understand. After all the things I've been used to! How could I give them all up just for my art? But families are all the same, aren't they? Just because they've lived in the same style and the same place for a few hundred years, they think their children have got to. That's why nice people, I mean people of nice family, start at such a disadvantage in the artistic world. One would much rather have been Duff or Varna.'

'But I thought Duff. . . .'

'Oh, don't you believe any of that; why, at Steubensville, Ohio, where I come from, the Duffs are very ordinary people.'

'Perhaps they aren't the same ones.'

'I tell you I know for certain – by the way, what is your name? – that my grandfather wasn't allowed to play with them. I don't know and don't care what's happened to them afterwards.'

'Well, families are a great nuisance, as you say.'

'Sure, and what's worse than a happy family, for that's what we were. Mother adored me, father adored me, all my brothers and sisters simply worshipped me. When I got married, my father said to my husband, "If you hurt one hair of head" – look, isn't it much quicker just to drink the stuff out of the bottle, I guess you're as tired as I am of putting water in and seeing it turn green – "well," he said, "you may be sure she comes of a long line of pure women and what-do-you-call-'em men." Does oo like little Ruby, please?'

'Like her, why, I think I'm a little in love with her.'

'Oh, you darling man – why do I live here, indeed! – I'll

tell you. Because it's so good for my daughter to be beside the sea. Now you know, Ruby's had a little daughter and she's not concealing anything from you – or is she, tee hee hee!'

'I'll have to find out when I know you better.'

'Tell me what you like in a woman.'

'Clean breath, firm breasts, and a flat stomach.'

'Well, you'll have to think up some other reasons for liking me then – don't you like a wife and a mother?'

'I like a wife and a mother.'

'An artist, a wife and a mother?' she continued. 'Why do you think there are so few good women composers?'

'I don't know, Ruby.'

'That's it. That's how I'm going to be famous, because there's so few women composers. Shall I play you something?'

'What's your favourite instrument?'

'Come over here and I'll show you.'

'When's your daughter coming back?'

'Oh, she's away at a convent. Duff put her into one.'

'Darling Ruby.'

'Now we'll close the door and start on the other bottle and little Ruby will tell you her life story.'

X

THE punishment of continual philandering, of trying to get every woman to have an affair with one, resides in the successes even more than in the failures. It is like playing with a revolver in which one of the chambers is loaded.

After a few days during which he gradually moved up to her place from the hotel, and during which they indulged in a perpetual absinthe dream, alternately holding each other's heads, Ruby fell violently in love with him. Several truths emerged. They were both miserably unhappy; both despised their way of life, only the other understood what they had been through, and together they would fight it. Next month, when he got his cheque and Ruby her alimony, they would set out, visit Paris, London, and America, and settle in the depths of a new country. For a day or two they drank plain soda water, went for walks, and together arranged his notes on Rogers. The albatross was round his neck again, and they discussed what would indubitably prove the *definitive* edition.

Suddenly they began to grow bad-tempered. An appalling fatigue descended on Naylor, a miserable depression, in which there united with the toxin, raging between his head and his stomach, the death throes of ambition – for it takes a long time to die, and to be stifled, like a shrimp in a sea-anemone, by the soft yielding amplexities of a woman in love was no pleasant end to it.

He began to make scenes, or when she asked him what was the matter to answer savagely, 'Oh, nothing you'd understand, merely a career wasted.'

'Well, I'm so dumb. Which one is it this time – the bar, the bench, the stock-exchange? It's always a seat on something I'm costing you. Even the can won't be safe next!'

'It's different for you. You're a musician, and it's possible to remain that indefinitely, as long as you don't risk a performance.'

'I do too – why my piano pieces were said by Antheil to be the most promising he had ever heard.'

'I know. I meant performance. Good God, have you ever met anybody who wasn't promising?'

'Now, I forbid you to speak to me like that. My brothers would have thrashed you.'

'Oh, I know all about it – the long line of plain women and queer men – they gave you everything except a face and a fortune.'

'Well, you're not so normal yourself. Why does every-body call you Queenie Manners, the lion-tamer? Don't kid yourself. Jimmy knows when a man's queer.'

'You rotten little piece of trash. Take that back im-mediately!'

'Oh, don't hit me, Edgar, I couldn't bear it.'

'I have no intention of hitting you.'

'But you are queer, aren't you? A woman knows.'

'If you say that again I'll slap your face.'

'Go on, you old English pansy. You're something out of a cottage garden.'

'I'll tell you one thing, Ruby, I might have got well, but you've got on my nerves so that I've been drinking for days down at the pub – so much for your woman's influence.'

'Well, so have I – and that's why I'm so sick of this might-have-been-anything talk – you male magnolia.'

He slapped her. She caught his hand and bit it. He hit her in the face with his disengaged fist and got both hands round her throat, shaking her little head up and down till the teeth rattled. 'I hate you – understand? I hate you', he hissed. Her arms clung round him, her eyes closed, drowsy with passion.

After such scenes they would find the days fuller, and Naylor would lie on the sofa while she cooked bacon and eggs. He rarely visited the hotel as Ruby's credit was better with the village wine shop, but once he went down and found three letters – the first was forwarded from Juan, a postcard from Spedding. 'Did you get my letter? What are these extraordinary stories we hear of you *via* Cambridge where one Foster, who has been seeing something of you, has written to the dean of Sidney Sussex? It appears Rogers goes a-Rogering in no uncertain fashion. *Mentula moecha-tur.*'

The next was also short:

37 bis impasse du Rouet.

Sir, I have been waiting impatiently for your quittance of the very
small amount owing to me. I must remind you that, however you
may choose to occupy your time, we artists are dependent on our
bread for our work.

To account.   One hundred francs.

Igor Andraievitch Rascasse.

Artiste-peintre.

The last was without date or address:

'Dear Naylor,

I want so much to write and thank you for how nice you were to
me down south. I had no idea a man could be so kind and good. I
mean a man *désinteressé*, you understand. I heard from Duff you
were not very well. I am sorry indeed and hope you will take care
of yourself. People always get so very ill when they are sick in
Trou. It is something in the mud or the water. We also have not
been having very happy times, and it seems as if things will never
be quite the same as at The Bastion. *Est-il déjà plus loin que
l'Inde ou la Chine?* – Charles Baudelaire.

First of all Varna left all her money in the toilette at Grez-sur-
Loing, Seine-et-Marne, I mean all her money from the bar. I went
back to look for it but nobody found anything except the empty
bag floating in the river. Then it seems the bookshops do not
want any assistants as they are getting rid of them now that so
few foreigners are left, so then I was offered a job on a paper to
pose for photographs in the nude, but it fell through as the man
was just a satyr. Then they asked me to wear clothes for a fashion
magazine and they were going to send me down to Cannes to try
on bathing dresses for the American Florida number, as there was
no sunshine for the photos nearer than Cannes, so I would have
seen you and Geraldine, but as the Customs would not let the
bathing dresses in they were sent back to America, and the
magazine decided it was better to have them photographed right
there in Florida, as the paper was so broke, and so that was off. I
couldn't stay with Varna any longer, and I can't go back to
Germany as I am not an Aryan, but, as you know, of Mongol
extraction, so I have got a job as hostess in a special boîte called

Chez la Reine Christine. There are six of us and we all wear dinner jackets with black skirts, which we pay for by instalments out of our wages. There are six other girls who are the cabaret and who are not allowed to wear dinner jackets; they are expected to dance with men also if requested. I know how you like to know all the details, so I will tell you that we get five francs on every drink that is bought at our table, dinner free, and a hundred francs a week. We usually get to bed about four, and have to be there about five o'clock in the afternoon – for the apéritif. One girl, a Hungarian, had her dinner jacket taken away for cheeking a client who turned out to be a famous American lady, and has had to work extra hours to win it back. It is quite comfortable but the stiff shirt is very cold. There are four in the band: the saxophone and the drums, who are both Roumanian girls, are a little bit in love with me. The manageress is an Italian. She is the most wonderful person I have ever met. Naturally a lot of our old Bastion friends call here. You heard about poor Princess Rustchuk? She quarrelled with her friend about not being allowed to speak to me and the friend went off with one of the dancers – the dark one who danced *Judith et Holopherne* – so Princess Rustchuk took the blonde to live with her, but found she had a girl who couldn't cook and the dancer a partner who couldn't dance, so they both had to give up the restaurant and the theatre and come to Paris. Now Princess Rustchuk comes here every night, and is always trying to talk to me, but she does not seem the same woman as at Saint-Pierre. It was all just a dream. Poor Geraldine has gone back to her family in England, since they took Dicky to the home. Rascasse hasn't had his exhibition – he asked too much for all his pictures – he wanted three thousand francs for your portrait and then he said the gallery weren't paying him a large enough commission. Poor Rascasse, he will never understand business. He is going to write – he is devoted to you. Sonia is in Munich but she finds it very boring. I saw Jimmy and Tahiti and her husband. They often come here. Lola has gone back to being a model – everyone is very broke, and it is very cold and wet; we are all afraid of the grippe and envy you down at Trou. When shall we meet again? Will you come ever to Montparnasse? How is your book? Mind you get well. Do you mind not showing

this letter about to people as myself, Rascasse and Lola have not
paid our rent and we do not want them to find us. Thank you
again very much for being so good to me. *Nous ne sommes pas
heureux à notre âge.* – Louis Quatorze.

From your loving Toni.

He walked up the hill with the letter, stopping to ex-
ecute one or two small commissions, a long French loaf at
the baker's (the most reassuring of childhood smells), a
couple of bottles of Pernod in the épicerie with its tins of
sardines and tunny, its strings of onions and sliced saus-
ages on the counter. 'For she my mind hath so displaced',
he remembered it now, 'that I shall never find my home.'
Did she wear a stiff or a soft collar? It was getting dark; in
the village houses he saw the charcoal fires gleaming on
the stone flags. The air was keen and damp – pinewoods,
burning oil, winter. One lived, however unprofitably; one
loved, or ceased to love; one changed, or did not change. He
was fairly patient with Ruby that evening – she was doing
her best – but what a drab, hysterical, juicy little beast! She
drank with him, but not too much (when one has something to give one's generation, she explained, it's one's
duty to keep sober), and indulged in day-dreams of the kind
of house they would have – 'a big room to work in, a real
studio, another for you to write in and everybody who was
doing interesting things to come to us and talk about them
and everybody who was in a jam or was broke'.

'Nonsense, you'd only want duchesses.'

'That's where you're so English. Can't you see that once
you've *been* someone you can't be interested in other
people just because they *are* someone. You're only
interested in people who do things because you yourself do
things.'

'Yes, darling, what a little thinker you are.'

'I know these things, you see, just as I knew when I was

127

playing that afternoon that I must stop and go to the door.
There's fate at the door. You see, I knew.'

'Bedtime soon.'

'Just turn the other way till little Ruby gets into bed.'

It was ten o'clock. He thought – the clients were just
beginning to arrive *Chez la Reine Christine.*

As he lay on the farthest verge of his corner of the iron
bed, under a petrol-scented army blanket, listening to
Ruby's breathing, the crackling of the charcoal stove and
the faint vibrations of the autumn silence, he tried for the
first time to think what his new life meant to him. He was
living with Ruby, on her alimony; in love with Tahiti or
something not unlike it, yet capable of receiving from
Toni a violent emotional shock. Even to Rascasse and
Jimmy, though not his friends, he was mysteriously
attached. Was this the lesson of Trou? That there were
intimacies closer than those based on respect and affection, qualities of mind which became indispensable, ties
that united these few last sad rebels, their possession of the
tragic sense of life perhaps, or of the happiness of the
moment? What had in fact happened? He knew only that
he was no longer the same fine specimen of English
pseudo-virginity, the Wykehamist who had arrived a few
weeks ago. The warring elements of lust and snobbery had
been melted down. He loved Toni without wanting to
sleep with her. For the first time he had enjoyed a natural
relationship with someone and had not snapped at them
like a trapped fox – and now he even lived with Ruby
without the constant indulgence of his sense of sin – while
from Tahiti he had learnt that his subconscious feeling
that he could buy women entitled him to buy only one
thing. And what was more, he had grown to like the troglodytes, these fierce, unfashionable expatriates. What was
fine in them, their refusal to conform, their independence,
their moral courage, was their own; what was weak, their

instability, hopelessness and predatory friendships, was
the result of a system: of the clumsy capitalist world that
exalts money-making and poisons leisure, that suppresses
talent, starves its artists, and persecutes its sexual dissen-
ters, that denies opportunity, infects charity, and encour-
ages only the vulgarity of competition, the triumphs, the
suspicion, the heart-break of the acquisitive life. 'Do, do,
what does he do? What is he doing now?' He remembered a
criticism of Ruby's: 'The trouble with you, Edgar, is that
all you English boys are brought up on marks. You say you
got marks for learning the collect, whatever that is, marks
for taking out the best books from the library, marks for
good conduct, for scholarships and examinations. Marks
for every time you opened your mouth till you left Oxford,
and now that they've stopped giving them, you don't know
what to do.'

But if he were like that, how much more so were his
friends. Could he ever go back among those galley slaves?
He thought of the dry kind who were ossifying into security as fast as they could, of the young barristers, publishers,
civil servants and Conservative candidates all in various
stages of snobbery, the true *maladie anglaise*. They all
seemed to be playing a game of grandmother's steps, in
which, whenever he looked round at them, they were
somehow blandly and innocently nearer the social success
which was their universal goal. And their vulgarity and
pot-boiling, their rowdy charm, taking small liberties with
each other, to see if they could get away with them, calling
each other old so-and-so, since 'old' implied impotence;
elbowing like tadpoles in a jar! And their self-important
belief in ghosts, saying of a great house where they had
spent a week-end, 'of course, it's terribly haunted'; their
implication that they could not afford to quarrel or make
enemies, that all that kind of thing was rather silly, their
mistaking of verbal twists for epigrams, of epigrams for

wit; products of a system of education which had sent
them out into the world with the opportune belief that
there existed to every worthwhile experience a short cut
which, like the back way into their colleges, they alone
knew how to take – and their smell of self-advancement,
like the stench that rises from publishers' advertisements
on Sunday mornings! Slaves too dull to feel their own
shackles, conceited termites! Yet how he would have liked
to be of these worldlings, elastic, adaptable, mercenary,
easily pleased! It was not his own wish but an ineluctable
growth inside that had separated him, fencing him off from
their company. He perceived that after adolescence, a time
when people are afraid of not feeling things enough, a time
when they dare not rely on their emotions, there comes a
period of silent change when a hereditary figure, a creature
of no self-expression or self-knowledge, but adamant and
invincible, rises slowly to the surface and begins to operate, forcing the young man who only affected to dislike
stupidity in films and plays actually to get up and leave in
the middle of them, or the youth, who ran up bills as if
Bond Street were his Christmas tree, into a long, slow
wooing of Maid Solvency – the paternal virtues stealthily
undermining the extravagances of the son. In the case of
Naylor, his focus had improved, an understanding had
come about between his awareness of beauty and his sense
of satire. He thought of his past. It had kept badly. Something in it, apparently wholesome at the time, had turned
in retrospect like milk in a thunderstorm. In adolescence
his desire for experience had been greater than his capacity
for it, every sensation, every intimacy had been slightly
stretched and inflated; art had always been overdrawn on
life, and the extent to which those scenes had been over-
acted was the extent to which they now seemed embarrassing and insincere. Now he was rid of that awkward, unde-
cided moodiness, out of the cycle of self-love, hate, self-

pity, and dimly he was aware of being hewn and hacked at, in that part of him which was most malleable, by some ferocious, feudal, iconoclast ancestor.

And now that the emotional content of his mind had been purified, could he not write better? Or would whatever he wrote remain subject to the laws which governed the young Englishman's first novel and made it a slop-pail for sex, quotations and insincerity? He was, he supposed, still irretrievably committed to the central concept of the nineteen-twenties – futility, the problem of the clever young man and the dirty deal, of the sensitive clown, the Petroushka, done down and cut out by his rival the Harlequin, the Moor, and, finally, too late, turning into the Moor.

Yes, why should he ever go back? He thought of the B.B.C., the *Daily Express, Nash's Magazine*, Sloane Street, the phosphorescent glow over the West End on Saturday nights, the loud greetings, the boasting of his friends, the culture, the teacake, how he would feel slightly iller every day, from gin and asphalt-poisoning, and slightly more rejected, for if sex and snobbery, at which he was a failure, were going out, he was no better fitted for the Communism and hope that were coming in. But here in Trou lay maturity, the rhythm of contrast that determined his being. The orchestra were taking their seats. So far his life had only been the scraping and shuffling, the false starts, the unpleasant toots and groans of tuning-up. Now it was going to break into a symphony, quiet at first, then infinitely broad and complicated, like a river that lingers, on its way to annihilation, over dappled reaches of stickle against a ground-bass of quiet pools.

The last expatriate! *Ultimus Romanorum!* And, besides, he loved this country. He began to be aware that the climate was not one of uniform sunshine, not merely lotophagous, but a succession of bright days and rainy calms, of exhilarating gales, before the wet and windy elegiacs of autumn subsided into winter, a winter already implicit with spring. And the land with its variety of altitudes, with its roomy hinterland of sea-green pine forest and Saracen hill-village, was unspoilt and bracing. Tomorrow he would walk up to La Gaude. And if he stayed long enough, they would all come back again, Toni and Tahiti, and Rascasse, and the owners of the Bastion. By then, Time, the humane killer, would have put an end to his sufferings. There were many women, many bars, many beaches, and he would no longer be tormented by bare knees and cool forearms, images glimpsed in the crypts of summer darkness under the planes. But he was forgetting Toni. Now she would be putting the studs in her shirt, brushing her hair, tying the laces of her patent leather shoes, arranging her tie. In the Djem el Fna, at Marrakesh, it would also be dark. The Chleuh boys, members of that rebel tribe whose maidens required a French soldier's testicles from every suitor, would be dancing on their dusty pitch, the silver castanets on their fingers, the huge ring on each left ear. The archaic music would be scraped out as they bowed and jingled in their long robes. There was a kind of corrupt dignity in their defeat.

Next morning his nerves were not so good. Regeneration does not come quickly, and the drafts of night are seldom honoured by the grim cashier of day. Living in close proximity with someone he did not love had brought to the surface his latent hatred of women. They were creatures to be used, complimented, or even chivalrously adored – but not to be lived with. The disarray of feminine garments in which he had to seek his own, the sloppiness, the lack of angles in any room which one shared with a woman, aroused in him an antithesis of prickly resentment. He clipped his words, flexed his wrists and fingers, opened and shut the drawers with a neat click. Dinner had not been washed up. There was a dirty plate on the floor by the bed. He went out to the pump for his shaving water. To be born again, to be born again! But where? In the Azores, perhaps. When he returned, feeling better for the fresh air, Ruby was playing. She had a high full little voice, like a bullfinch.

Like the beat, beat, beat of the tom-tom
In the jungle afternoon,
Like the drip, drip, drip of the raindrops
When the summer's shower is through.

'Please don't, do you mind?'

So a voice within me keeps repeating: 'You, you, you'.

'Stop it, will you?'

Night and day – day and night – under the hide of me
With an, oh, such a yearning, burning feeling inside of
me.

He performed the awkward gesture known as banging down the keyboard.

'Why, what's the matter? It's the only piece of jazz I like.'

'Don't play it. It has unpleasant associations for me.' He did indeed think for a moment of that disturbing exotic tune as he had heard it under the vines on his first evening.

'I've yet to find anything in your existence that wasn't an unpleasant association. Perhaps that's why you've got so many friends.'

'One day I'll kill you.'

'Queenie!'

'Besides, I have got a friend. I had a very nice letter from one yesterday evening.'

'May one ask who it is?'

'Certainly. There were three. Rascasse, John Spedding –

who's doing very well in the sort of job I should be having if I went back now – and little Toni.'

'Well, she used to be a friend of mine.'

'I've never seen you together.'

'She was very fond of me indeed.'

'–!'

'She was! We had an affair together.'

'She was in love with Princess Rustchuk.'

'That's the point. She mistook me for her one day and for a couple of weeks I lived in the borrowed aura, if you understand.'

'I see – who else have you lived with?'

'Only her and Eddie.'

'Eddie-from-the-top?'

'Yes, you heard me. I was living with him when I met Toni. It was he named the house. When I met Toni he got mad and left me. That's how he came to fall for Lola. He'd never have had a knife in him if he'd stayed with me.'

'No, but you would.'

'Now, Edgar, don't be cheap.'

'So it was Toni, eh!'

'What was?'

'You filthy little wretch!'

'Oh, Edgar, you aren't jealous. I never loved her like I love you. It's quite a different thing with a woman. Besides, Duff says she's stolen all the profits from the bar. She's just an adventuress.'

'You believe that?'

'Of course I do – I promise I do. She's just a common thief. Don't look so terrible, Edgar. It's all over now. It was all over the moment I saw you.'

'So you think she's a thief – what a wonderful lover – why, even if she is a thief she's a thousand times more honest than you'll ever be!'

'Oh, don't strike me.'

'Not a chance, this time – you can't be honest about your birth, your music, your looks, your daughter, about liking me to hit you; you're rotten all through, the rottenest thing in this rotten place. You stink of cheap middle-class hypocrisy.'

'Aren't you behaving rather like that game-keeper, Queenie?'

'All right, you fat leech, you blood-sucking little sheep-tick!'

'You're drunk.'

'No, I'm not – it's *you* who's drunk.'

'Not by *your* standards.'

'I'll kill you.'

'Yes. You'll kill me, and you'll write a wonderful book about that fairy hero of yours and you'll be a stockbroker and you'll go on taming women because you've such a way with you, and getting put out of other people's cars, and being sentimental about everybody till they're sick of you gooing over them, and then you'll think you've been badly treated. "I've never had a proper break" – I know that gag. At least the rest of us here drink because we like it; you turn it into going to church. I don't care if you do like women – you're queer – one part, if you can call it a part of you, is normal – but all the rest of you is queer. You're just a pansy that's gone wrong. You can't even be a proper pansy. Yes, sir, you're just an old hit-me-again in a whack-house.'

He picked up a plate and threw it at her. It hit her just above the eye. The bottle missed. The broken tumbler made a jagged cut on the side of the throat. She slumped over, upsetting the table. Blood and Pernod ran down his manuscript on to the floor. 'Rogers himself was fond of quoting opinions of his own achievements,' he read, 'such as Mason's on his *Italy*: "I thought it a good subject carefully composed, and indeed none of us could have written so well," and Crowe's: "I cannot find in your versification anything to mend".'

He looked spellbound at the lines and tried to convince himself that nothing else existed. Versification, indeed! Then the blood soaked into them. He rushed forward. He had killed her. It would mean 'the Widow' for this. The last cigarette, the glass of rum. *'Courage, Naylor, votre dernière heure est venue!'* The carriage in which one drives to the guillotine returns as a hearse.

The cut had stopped bleeding. She opened her eyes. 'Oh, Edgar!'

This time he was through, finished. He strode down the hill to the café. This time she had gone too far. She had ruined his manuscript. She had said unforgivable things. He ordered a double whisky. This was the extremity of squalor. Would she be such a fool as to cook any luncheon?

Some new people came into the bar – two young men and a woman. They were well dressed, handsome, and ordered their drinks in English. They little knew! Poor innocents! They little knew! They hadn't, like he, ruthlessly analysed the iniquity of the place, upturned all its messy little love affairs and sordid histories. He must warn them. He got up and tottered to the bar.

'Excuse me, I heard you talking English. I just wanted to say that I should strongly advise you not to stay here. It's an unhealthy hole at the best of times, and quite empty just as present.'

'Thanks very much. Have a drink?'

'A double whisky.'

They did not look at him while he held out his hand.

'Of course, it's quite all right if you meet only a few people,' he went on silkily. 'If you're staying all day you must come and lunch with me, and I'll show you how to find your way about.'

Frank open look: preferably at girl: whoopee: an eructation.

'I'm sure we'd have loved to', she answered, 'but I don't think we're stopping.'

Long walk back to table. Do things carefully. Put the glass down. So. Now sit in chair. One at a time though. Careful. So. Put legs out. Left, right. Big magic. Whoopee. Made three faces turn a kind of red at a distance of several yards. Big magic.

I shall live in a Palladian house set among wind-blown lagoons. A palace on the Lima or the river of Collares. There will be columns, statues, tall windows, baroque saloons in dust-sheets, a garden reservoir full of slime and lilies. There I shall cultivate obscurity and practise failure, so repulsive in others, in oneself of course the only dignified thing. 'My baptismal name is Aegeus' – his mutter was quite audible. 'That of my family I will not mention, but no towers in the land are more time-honoured than my gloomy grey hereditary halls.'

Phew! Edgar Poe! Edgar Naylor!

The three strangers left with a nod. They seemed to be discussing someone. 'Just another bum, Jane.' He heard the dark girl's low reply 'I think he's kind of cute.' Then the noise of a car starting.

How true it was! What a good description of the local expatriate. He would try it out on Ruby about Eddie. It fitted old Rascasse too. And Jimmy. And Foster. All the bloody lot. He saw Ruby come bobbing down the hill in her red sweater. Her face was bandaged. Eddie would be out of hospital pretty soon. Yes, yes. There were many women, many beaches, many bars. This was the soul's February. Outside all was bleak and unpromising, but deep within him stirred something unexpected, something noble. He considered the rows of coloured bottles – Cassis, Mandarinette, Cordial Médoc. A thousand-franc note, and in the corner he would write: 'For my darling Toni'.

A *ten* thousand-franc note!

'Hey! GarÇON!' No use. Just another bum, indeed!

I wonder.